Finding Clara

By

Jannie Lund

Published by
Satin Romance
An Imprint of Melange Books, LLC
White Bear Lake, MN 55110
www.satinromance.com

ISBN: 978-1-68046-148-0

Cover Art by Stephanie Flint

Thank You:

Lisbeth Pihl Lerche, for knowing twenty years ago that I'd end up being immensely grateful for learning those pesky irregular verbs by heart. I often think of you when I write.

Heather Upton and Lashawn Hubenak, for an alternative and (almost) always enjoyable comma education.

Nancy Schumacher, for continuing to believe in me.

Stephanie Flint, for reading my mind and improving on the images you find in there.

Anna Grethe Lund, for being on my side always.

This book is for you.

Chapter One

Clara studied the house as she walked past it again. It looked just as intimidating as it had the first time. The house itself looked beautiful and almost friendly with the colorful front yard full of asters and the vines climbing the white walls. However, what the house represented, scared Clara enough to keep walking until she reached the end of the street. Pretty soon, someone would notice her walking back and forth and call the cops. Luckily, they knew she was there. There was a park across the road, and Clara decided to go there to gather her courage, which really meant that she was going there to procrastinate.

She sat down on a bench and watched the people passing by—an elderly couple walking arm in arm, a boy on his bike, a woman with a stroller. They all looked so content, while Clara felt uneasy in her own skin. She was a coward. She should have stopped at the house the first time she'd reached it. She should have rung the doorbell so the people inside would be put out of their misery.

Taking a deep breath in a futile attempt to steady her nerves, she thought back over the past months. It felt like she hadn't been herself since that night in July when she'd abruptly ended a phone conversation with a friend. She'd been watching the news when life as she knew it had come to a noisy stop. Since then, she'd barely been able to do her job— teach the wonderful kids at the high school, who lived and breathed art like she did herself—nor had she picked up a paintbrush.

Frustrated, she rubbed her mitten-clad hands over her thighs. She'd begged the sheriff for the opportunity to confront her unknown family alone. By sitting in the park, she was abusing his trust in her and prolonging the grief of the people in the house on the hill.

Clara was usually only bold when she swung her paintbrushes over a canvas. Otherwise, she wasn't very brave, but now she needed courage to get through what awaited her. She held the power to alter not only her own life, but also the life of an unknown family, and it was high time she used that power for something—hopefully something good.

Reluctantly, she rose from the bench. No matter how long she waited, she would never be truly ready. With determination she had to conjure with her imagination, she marched back up the road and turned into the flower-lined path leading up to the house. Even though early fall had arrived, asters still bloomed. On the front porch, there were pots with heather and boxwood. The light was on above the door even though it was the middle of the afternoon. Clara knew why—the sheriff had told her—it broke her heart and made her even more uneasy.

With what was supposed to be a deep but ended up a very shallow breath, she rang the doorbell, startled when she heard it chime inside. Even after all this time, she still wasn't completely sure what to say. A woman her own height with dark hair peppered with a little gray in a loose bun opened the door. She was wearing an apron over slacks and a dark green sweater.

"Can I help you?"

Clara's thoughts were racing a million miles per hour in her head. "Um, I hope so. My name is Clara Christensen. I'm looking for Grace and Carl Quinn."

"I'm Grace. Come on inside, dear. Carl is in his office, I'll just go get him. Are you one of his students?"

Clara shook her head. This woman was her mother, although putting such a title on an unknown woman seemed ridiculous. "Oh, no. I just... I just need to talk to the two of you if that's okay. I can come back if this is a bad time."

Grace Quinn smiled pleasantly. "Now is fine. I'll just get Carl. If you want, you can leave your jacket on the chair and wait in the living room. It's just through there."

"Thank you, ma'am." She'd only been in America a few days, but the 'sir's' and 'ma'am's' came naturally to her already. Back home, everything was less formal.

Mrs. Quinn smiled again and left her to walk down a long hallway. Clara took off her jacket and put it down. She took a look around before entering the living room. It was a beautiful home, big, spacious and

2

thoughtfully decorated. Deep, comfortable-looking furniture in dark wood, a lot of glass and matching colors in white, brown, dark red and green. Out of instinct, her eyes flew almost immediately to the artwork on the walls, and the sight of the oil paintings, pencil sketches and watercolors made her relax a little. This she knew and could relate to. Everything else…

Mrs. and Mr. Quinn came into the living room. Clara struggled to swallow. She had to try three times before she managed it. She was aware that she was staring at them while Mrs. Quinn did the introductions and asked her to sit down. Mr. Quinn was a tall, broad man, also with dark hair. He had mostly grayed, though, and his eyes were a startling green.

"So what can we do for you, dear?"

Mrs. Quinn's friendliness was a little over the top and familiar at the same time. Clara's grandmother had been the same way, always inviting people into her home and going out of her way to help everyone.

Clara dismissed the memories. She needed to find the right words— there would be no do-over if she screwed it up. "Even though I've thought about nothing else lately, I still don't know how to start, so I apologize in advance if I get ahead of myself telling you what I have to say. Maybe letting you know that Sheriff Jameson knows I'm here is the best start. In fact, he's the one who gave me permission. Also your address."

"Sheriff Jameson…" Mrs. Quinn turned pale and gripped her husband's hand.

Wringing her own hands, Clara knew she should put them out of their misery, but finding the words was difficult. Maybe she should have let Sheriff Jameson tag along like he'd suggested, but she'd thought it too personal to have strangers—*more* strangers—involved. "Will you bear with me if I start at the beginning?"

"Of course," Mr. Quinn replied.

Mrs. Quinn just nodded and clung to her husband's hand.

Clara took a deep breath and forced herself to relax her tightly fisted hands. "About two months ago, there was a story on the news in Denmark—that's where I'm from—about a well-known lawyer who had committed suicide. He'd left a confession of sorts behind, and the police released the contents of that confession to the media. For almost forty years, he had been involved in international organized crime involving what you could call 'white laundering kidnapped children' so that unsuspecting couples adopted them legally. When I watched that news segment, I recognized the lawyer's name because I'd seen it on my own adoption papers."

"Eve…" Mrs. Quinn whispered almost in awe while Clara tried not to flinch at the sound of the name.

"Ssshh. Don't get ahead of yourself, Grace," Mr. Quinn said gently, but he never took his eyes off Clara. "Please continue."

She wanted to let Mrs. Quinn out of her agony, but she knew that if she did, she'd never get to finish her story. "I did some research on the case. I talked to the police, checked the church records, that sort of thing. My birth certificate turned out to be fake. The police kind of pushed me to the back of the line when it came to opening a 'cold' case, as they had others with easier leads. The first thing they wanted to do was talk to my parents about their memories of the adoption. But they passed away a few years ago and without them, I guess it was too difficult. I was told that they'd look into my case once they'd gotten leads in some of the other 'easier' cases."

Clara looked away from the tense couple on the opposite side of the coffee table. She didn't know them or their pain, but she could feel part of it anyway.

"So I started my own investigation. Using the clues I found in the media, I thought I could solve the puzzle myself. But I couldn't. Instead, I hired a private investigator. I knew from the police that it wasn't just a Danish thing. There were more than a hundred cases they knew of at that point and they solved a few—a boy adopted by a Danish couple. The boy had been kidnapped in Spain. His mother was told by the hospital staff that he was stillborn and she couldn't see him because he was too deformed."

The story made tears run down her cheeks as it had the first time she'd heard it. She cleared her throat. "The private investigator based his search on my skin color and what I could tell him about dates and such. He came up with four alternatives pretty quickly. Four missing girls, born in 1986, who have never been found."

"Please," Mrs. Quinn whispered.

Clara nodded, feeling nauseous. "Your daughter was one of them. I contacted the police instead of the families, because I didn't want to upset anyone unnecessarily. Sheriff Jameson arranged for a DNA test."

She couldn't say the words. Instead, she reached for the report in her purse and handed it to Mr. Quinn. It was hard for her to watch as they studied it, knowing that they would find the news amazing, whereas Clara didn't know what to think. It was not good news, it was not bad news, it was just life-altering news.

It was like an out-of-body experience when Mrs. Quinn hugged her. There were tears, sobs, and praises to a God Clara wasn't sure she believed in. Mr. Quinn hugged her, too—almost desperately—and while Clara's brain could understand their relief, her heart was strangely disconnected. The fact that they called her 'Eve' didn't help any.

She wasn't Eve, at least she didn't feel like her. She hadn't missed Grace and Carl Quinn all her life. She hadn't even known they existed. She had looked at the DNA report again and again; it still hadn't changed anything for her. She felt horrible for being so cold and detached when the two people who had given her life had just gotten back the child they'd lost twenty-seven years ago.

"I can't believe it. I've hoped and prayed for this moment so many times. All the different outcomes..." Mrs. Quinn stared at Clara to the point where she was uncomfortable. She kept touching her, too, as if to make sure that she was real. "I was so afraid this day would never happen. I even lost hope sometimes."

Clara couldn't stop the tears. Mrs. Quinn, who hadn't stopped crying herself, hugged her again. "It's okay. Everything is going to be okay now."

The words made Clara cry even harder. She was embarrassed when she pulled back. "I'm sorry."

Brilliant smiles met her uncertain gaze. "Don't apologize for tears."

Clara bit the inside of her cheek. How could she possibly explain that it wasn't the tears but the big, empty void inside of her for which she was apologizing?

"I can't believe you're here." Mrs. Quinn smiled and wiped her eyes. "You're so beautiful, like you were as a baby. You look like

Rachel. I should have noticed it, but I've had to teach myself not to hope that every girl who looked a little bit like Rachel was you."

Clara didn't know who Rachel was, but Mr. Quinn was apparently a bit more levelheaded than his wife was at that point. "Did Jameson tell you anything about our family?"

"Not really. Just the basics of the case." Which hadn't been much. Apparently, the only witness had been a little boy who had seen a woman in a car.

"Rachel is your little sister. You have three brothers, too. Practically four."

At Clara's no doubt confused look, Mr. Quinn elaborated. "Duncan. He's not ours by blood or name, but we love him as much as the others."

Siblings. Clara closed her eyes briefly. How many times growing up had she wished for siblings? Now that she was given four, practically five, she felt like it was too much.

"There is so much to tell you," Mrs. Quinn said, laughing shakily. "And so many things I want to ask. I don't even know where to begin."

Once again, Mr. Quinn was able to think clearer. "How about a cup of coffee and one of those cookies you were making, Grace? I'm sure Eve needs to catch her breath as much as we do." He smiled. "It's a big day."

Clara winced at being called Eve, but none of them seemed to notice. Mrs. Quinn kissed her on the cheek, whispering an almost silent and reverent, *"My daughter,"* and went to get coffee and cookies.

"I'm sorry your adoptive parents passed away," Mr. Quinn said. "All these years... I've always hoped and prayed that you were alive, that someone was taking good care of you."

"They did." Clara could smile now, thinking about Birthe and Erik Christensen, who would always be her parents in her heart. "When I was twelve, they told me I was adopted, but that it only meant they loved me because they couldn't help themselves—not because they *had* to."

Then she surprised herself with her candor. "They would have been horrified if they'd known their happiness was at another family's expense."

Mr. Quinn grabbed her hand and squeezed it. The look in his eyes was kind. "You said yourself that they didn't know, so they're hardly to blame. As long as you're happy, they'd be happy. It's how any parent would think."

She nodded, feeling incredibly awkward again. She didn't know what to say to this man who was her father, according to a DNA report.

Mr. Quinn rose to grab a large, framed photograph from the mantle. He sat down again next to her and held the photo so she could see it. It was a family portrait.

"That there is our oldest, Benjamin. Vanessa, his wife, next to him and their kids, Tommy and Leanne. They're four and two. Cutest things I ever saw. And our second oldest, Daniel and his wife, Linda."

Benjamin and Daniel looked a lot alike—tall, lean, dark-haired men with green eyes. Benjamin was impeccably dressed in a dark suit. His hair was short. Daniel, on the other hand, looked more rugged. He had longer hair and whiskers, his clothes were colorful and there was a hole in his jeans. There was something about him that looked familiar, but she dismissed the thought. Vanessa was a pretty redhead, and the kids had inherited their mother's hair and their father's eyes. Like Mr. Quinn had said, they were cute. Daniel's wife Linda was a tall blonde. She looked a little intimidating.

"That's Lucas," Mr. Quinn continued, stealing glances at her all the time. "You and he are twins. The white rose he's holding is for you. He always insists on having one in official family portraits. He's…"

"Yes?" Clara found the thought of a twin more exciting than she wanted to admit.

Mr. Quinn smiled almost sadly. "He's always claimed to know that you were alive, even when the rest of us sometimes lost hope. He's taken some heat for it, too. He's never been afraid of telling people he could somehow feel you out there somewhere. They haven't always been very understanding."

Clara looked at the picture again. A twin. A brave twin at that.

"And then there's Rachel. You can probably see that you look a lot alike."

"Yes." Clara wanted to feel some kind of kinship with this unknown sister, but it was all in her head. "How old is she?"

"Twenty-one. She's in college. These days she wants to study psychology, but she changes her mind a lot." He laughed softly. "Next to

7

her in the picture is Duncan. He wasn't blessed with parents who knew how to appreciate a child, so we've done our best to give him what he needed over the years. We couldn't love him any more if he'd been ours by blood."

A little of the ice in Clara's heart melted. Grace and Carl Quinn had essentially done what Birthe and Erik Christensen had—taken in a child who needed love. She looked at the picture and felt her heart stutter.

Duncan was a little taller than the Quinn men were and had darker hair. His eyes were clear blue and while the others in the photo were smiling, he appeared to be laughing. Clara could only describe him as beautiful. She could also describe him as an asshole. An asshole who had broken her heart more than she had ever wanted to admit to herself. It was not only a small world—it was a microscopic world. Determined not to think of him more than necessary, she looked away. Admitting to Mr. Quinn how she knew Duncan Cantwell was definitely a story for another time. Preferably never.

Her eyes drifted back to the white rose. She'd had a place in this unknown family all along. Although she could only imagine what it was like to have a baby daughter or sister go missing, she almost wished that she *had* known about it. At least then, she would have been better able to relate.

"You have a beautiful family, Mr. Quinn," she said truthfully.

"Thank you." He looked hurt despite her compliment. It took her a moment to realize why. To him, she was *Eve*. To her, he was *Mr. Quinn*. Neither liked those titles. However, before she could think of anything to say that would diffuse the situation, a frantic-looking man came running in. She recognized him from the portrait as Lucas. The twin. *Her* twin.

"Mom? Dad? She's close! I can feel her." He stopped abruptly as he spotted Clara on the couch next to his father.

Mrs. Quinn came running. "Luke?"

Lucas never took his eyes off Clara, who had to dig her fingernails into her palms not to squirm. "Eve," he whispered, unprompted.

Chapter Two

Every time someone called her 'Eve', it made the hole in her heart bigger—the hole that had appeared when she'd realized her life had been a lie, a deception.

"My name is Clara." Her voice was surprisingly strong. As pride seeped through her for being strong when she thought she couldn't be, she also instantly regretted it. It wasn't their fault that she was on a different frequency than they were. "I'm sorry. I just can't pretend to have a different name."

She couldn't read the expressions on Mrs. and Mr. Quinn's faces, but Lucas offered her an impossibly wide smile.

"Hello, Clara. It doesn't really matter what your name is," he said and closed the distance between them. "You're exactly who you're supposed to be, which is *you*. I've missed the hell out of you."

He gave her a bone-crushing hug, and even though his words confused her, she hugged him back. She could honestly say that she missed what he could have been to her the past twenty-seven years. She had a very distinct feeling that they had both missed out on a lot. For some reason, he made everything more real, even though she couldn't put her finger on why.

"I'm Luke, by the way. We shared a womb."

Her laugh was unexpected, and it made him smile again. "God, I can't believe you're here. Something inside of me told me you were close, but I hadn't expected to find you here."

It was strange to hear him talk about the connection or whatever it was so casually. If it was true—and she'd read about twins having weird connections—then why hadn't she ever felt something? Or known he was out there?

"Why didn't you call and tell me?" he asked, turning to face his dad.

"I was at work, and it hit me like a bad migraine that E—sorry, Clara, was close."

"She rang the doorbell less than an hour ago, son." Mr. Quinn smiled at Clara, who had to admit that as far as unknown fathers went, he seemed to be okay.

Clara had to retell her story for Lucas, and then twice more when Benjamin, Daniel, Rachel and Duncan came by. Apparently, Lucas had wasted no time texting his siblings, although Mrs. Quinn wasn't impressed with him sharing such important news via a simple text message.

Daniel was loud, boisterous and generous with hugs, smiles and laughter. Benjamin was quieter, but he nearly crushed her with his hug. Rachel couldn't stop crying and laughing. Clara could barely understand a word she was saying. Duncan did a visible, at least to her, double take when he recognized her, but thankfully didn't say anything. Instead, he welcomed her to the family, but other than that, he seemed content to watch everyone with a fond smile on his face. It was weird. She hated that he looked as sinfully good as the last time she'd seen him. She shouldn't have cared, much less noticed—not when he'd left her with a bruised and scarred heart. Ideally, she would have ignored him completely, but that would have been too weird, and the last thing she wanted was to explain.

They all fussed, asked questions and told her things that didn't stick in her mind. Clara felt like running away. In the days that had passed since she discovered she had once been Eve Quinn, she thought a lot about her unknown family—what they might be like and how they would react to her showing up after so many years. She had not been prepared to feel so overwhelmed, though. They were all big on touching, holding her hand, hugging her, but they were missing a very important point. She was a stranger. They were strangers to her.

Benjamin and Daniel's wives, as well as Benjamin's children also showed up for the impromptu dinner Mrs. Quinn produced. It was clear they had dropped everything to come rushing to the Quinn house as soon as they'd seen Lucas' text.

"I can't believe you're really here," Rachel told Clara while they ate. "Growing up, the boys have been grounded so many times for teasing me because I was the only one who'd never met you."

Clara didn't know how to respond. Apologize for being kidnapped? Her head was pounding, and her brain felt like it had been fried. Luckily, Mr. Quinn cleared his throat and asked for everyone's attention, so she could just smile meekly at Rachel.

"We have hoped and prayed and dreamed of this day for twenty-seven years," Mr. Quinn said slowly, looking around the table. He smiled gently, settling his gaze on Clara. "It has been a long and hard wait, difficult to keep hoping sometimes, but now we know that our beautiful girl is alive, safe, happy and she's back with us. I think it's safe to say that this day will forever be one of the greatest in the history of the Quinn family."

The silence that followed was serene until Clara realized they were all looking at her. To her great embarrassment, she felt tears threatening to escape but she managed to blink them away.

It seemed to take forever for the silence to end. Clara was relieved when Daniel started questioning her about where she lived in Denmark.

"Copenhagen," she replied. "I grew up north of the city but now I live in the actual city."

"Linda and I lived there for three years," he told her, wistfully. "We might have passed each other on the street..."

That's when it hit her why he seemed so familiar. She wasn't a big soccer fan, but she had seen the local team play a few times. She'd seen Danny Quinn, nicknamed 'US Air Force' by the fans, in action. Her unknown brother.

"I didn't even realize before now... I've seen you play a few times when my friends dragged me to a game. I saw the one where you were injured."

"God, I wish I'd known that. My career ended that day, but it wouldn't have meant a damn thing if only..." He shook his head. "So many cases of 'if only' in this family. Ben and Luke have spent most of their lives playing the 'if only' game."

She didn't ask him to elaborate. It was probably none of her business. At least she told herself she didn't want it to be.

As the evening progressed, Clara felt more and more beside herself—detached from what was going on around her. She tried to keep a smile on her face, but she couldn't stand the happiness. She understood it but it rubbed her heart raw. It was nearing midnight when Vanessa and Ben left with their sleeping children and everyone else followed reluctantly, after telling Clara they'd see her soon. Duncan gave her a strange look, one that held too many emotions for her to identify, before leaving. There was no doubt; a not very pleasant conversation with him was in her future.

"Are you sure you won't stay?" Mrs. Quinn asked for the fourth time. "There's always been a room ready for you."

"Thank you, but I don't feel right imposing."

"Oh, you wouldn't be, dear."

"It's really sweet of you, but I would feel like I was. I'm sorry."

Several hugs and promises later—Mrs. Quinn refused to let her leave before she'd agreed to come by for lunch the following day—Luke finally told his parents he had to get up early in the morning and since he was giving Clara a ride to her hotel, they had to go. She could have kissed him.

It wasn't until Clara had closed the hotel door behind her that she finally took the deep breath she had needed for hours. She was exhausted and wasted no time flopping on the bed, not even bothering to take off her jacket or shoes.

What a day. Even if she searched every dictionary in the world, she would never find a word to describe what she felt. Above all, she was relieved that the day was over and done with. Telling them, meeting them, seeing their reaction was what she'd feared the most. It made her feel bad that she couldn't share their joy, but she hadn't been waiting to reunite with them for twenty-seven years. She'd been half-dreading it for a little over a week.

The fact that two of them hadn't been complete strangers was weird. She had seen her brother before. Watched him play soccer while drinking draft beer and wishing she were somewhere else. And Duncan. She closed her eyes and tried to evict all thoughts of him from her mind. He was even more familiar, big asshole that he was. A vacation fling that she had obviously read too much into. Sighing, she admitted the truth to herself. He'd been more than a fling. Much more. She'd never connected with someone so fast before. Having lived with the knowledge that she'd

tell that you knew me."

"Mr. Quinn showed me a family portrait before you arrived, so I knew to expect you. I was mad at you." She sighed. "I also didn't think it was the right time to get into what happened between us."

"I agree. Truth be told, I can't stop feeling guilty. If I'd only figured out somehow that you were Eve back then."

"How could you? Sure, I look like Rachel, but so do a lot of other brunettes."

He didn't reply. "Come on. We're getting cold."

Annoyed, she followed him with a shake of her head as he started running back the same way they'd come from. *Wrong phone number my ass!* She was far from convinced.

They didn't speak on the way back, which Clara didn't mind too much. She took her running seriously, but she also took a lot of other things seriously, such as sleep and food. So while she loved running, she was never quite as in shape as she wanted to be. Sleep enticed her in the mornings too often, and sweets found permanent residence on her hips and thighs. It was the marathon of a lifetime. *Her* lifetime.

"That's Danny's car," Duncan told her when they slowed down in front of her hotel.

"Maybe he's stalking me, too."

He rolled his eyes at her but followed her inside. Danny was talking to the guy at the front desk, but left him without a second glance when he spotted Clara and Duncan. "There you are!"

"Good morning," Clara said, feeling a little crowded again. She had hoped her hotel would be her safe heaven. Apparently, that wasn't to be.

Danny pulled her into a hug. "Good morning. Hey, Dunc. What are you doing here?"

"I went for a run, met Clara, so we ran together."

"You live across town, dude. And your car is outside."

"So is yours."

Clara shook her head, wondering if they would even notice if she slipped away. Her exasperation grew when she saw Ben come out of the elevator.

"Oh, there you are. Good morning... Clara."

"Good morning." The smile she sent him was only half forced.

He, too, raised his eyebrows at seeing Duncan and soon, he was engaged in the why-are-you-here discussion.

Clara went over to the front desk and smiled at the guy there. "Hi. Sorry if...my brothers have been bothering you. They mean well, I think. When they come up for air, will you tell them that I'm in my room?"

He grinned. "Yes, ma'am."

"Thank you."

None of them noticed her leaving. She had showered and dressed before she heard a knock on the door.

Chapter Three

Surprisingly, it was Luke.

"Hi. I sent the hooligans downstairs home. They were disturbing the peace. They said to tell you that they were sorry, but older brothers are allowed to worry. Duncan said he'd be by later to give you a course in handwriting, whatever that means."

She couldn't help but smile. "Hi."

"Can I take you to breakfast? As an older brother, I'm apparently allowed to worry, and breakfast is the most important meal of the day."

"You're older than me?"

"Twenty long minutes to be exact."

"Huh. Good to know. Thank you."

As they walked to a nearby diner, Luke probed her about what Duncan said about handwriting.

"It's nothing. Just him thinking he's clever."

"If you say so." Luke offered her an easy grin like he didn't believe her, but she just rolled her eyes. She wished being around everyone in her new family was as easy as it was with Luke.

Luke ordered them a mountain of pancakes, which Clara eyed warily while inhaling her coffee. It was not the sort of breakfast she was used to, but when in Rome…or Connecticut…

"So tell me about everyone," she said. "There was so much talking yesterday, but I still don't know anything about anyone. What do you do for a living, for instance?"

"I took over an antiques store a couple of years ago, though it feels more like a souvenir shop sometimes the way the tourists make and break me. It's just down the street. I studied art history in college and was determined to prove that it wasn't a waste of time." He laughed and dug into his pancakes.

"That's cool. I can't wait to see it. Art history is never a waste of time. I teach art at a high school and spend most of my time painting. Well, I did. I've been so distracted lately that I've neglected my art."

"Twins separated for twenty-seven years both end up working with art. That's pretty amazing."

She smiled. "Yeah. It kind of is."

He smiled through another couple of mouthfuls of pancakes. "Ben works at a bank, as we've always known he would. As a kid, he actually enjoyed it when Mom made us wear ties."

Clara laughed and Luke continued. "Danny played soccer, as you know, but now he teaches PE at the high school. Linda also teaches— English. Vanessa is at home with the kids most of the time, but she works a few hours every week at a real estate office. Duncan is a photographer, Dad is a law professor at the college, although he doesn't work as much as he used to and Mom is also cutting back on her hours. She has a catering business."

Trying to mentally file everything, she nodded. There was a lot to keep track of.

"Do you know how long you're staying?" he asked.

She shook her head. "No. I...I don't know a whole lot at the moment. It feels like my life is up in the air. I'm just waiting for it to fall down so I can pick up the pieces and try to fit them together."

"I can't imagine what it's like for you. Right now, it's hard to see past the extreme happiness of having you back but that's part of the point, isn't it? We have you back. You don't have us *back*."

She nodded, fighting the tears. He did understand.

They talked a little longer then they walked to Luke's store. He showed it to her before he had to open and it was a little slice of paradise. She didn't know much about the antiques, but she loved looking at the artwork he had showcased. When customers started showing up, she said good-bye and set her course toward the sheriff's office. She'd promised Mrs. Quinn she'd come to lunch, but first she needed to pop in and see Sheriff Jameson.

It didn't take long to relay to the sheriff that she'd reconnected with her long lost family the previous day. He'd apparently gotten to know Mr. and Mrs. Quinn over the years, so he was happy it had worked out.

He told her he would get in contact with the Danish police and contact her if and when they made a breakthrough. Clara decided not to hold her breath.

Her next stop was the house on the hill again. She was almost as apprehensive as she'd been the day before. She hoped it was just a matter of getting to know them, but she wasn't able to relax around Mr. and Mrs. Quinn.

The first thing she noticed was that the porch light had been switched off. Sheriff Jameson had told her that it had been lit since the day she'd been kidnapped, as a beacon of hope and to let her know that if or when she ever returned, she was welcome. She swallowed hard as she thought about what it must have felt like to turn it off. She had to make more of an effort for her unknown parents.

It didn't matter which way you looked at it. She was their daughter. It wasn't their fault that she felt more like Clara than Eve. She didn't even know who Eve Quinn was. Imagining them as parents was hard, but she could at least be friendly…Open…Welcoming. *Try to connect with them.* She wouldn't always be dropping by for lunch every day. One day soon, she'd go back home and have to stay in touch via phone or e-mail. Maybe Skype. Visit sometimes. That would probably be easier. Until then, she would do her best to suck it up. If only they wouldn't call her Eve.

Rachel came running out to meet her. "Hey, Clara!"

"Hi." Clara managed a genuine smile. "Shouldn't you be at school?"

Laughing, Rachel grabbed Clara's hand. "You sound like a big sister already. Yes, I should. But spending time with you is more important."

Clara didn't mind Rachel being there. She didn't know why it was harder to be around Mr. and Mrs. Quinn than everyone else. It was like they expected her to be a certain way, a way she didn't even know. Rachel chattering excitedly was a great buffer.

* * * *

"I barely slept a wink last night," Mrs. Quinn said over the delicious lunch she'd made. "I was afraid I was going to wake up and discover that yesterday had been a dream."

Clara had a difficult time responding to statements like that. "I didn't sleep a lot either. There was—*is*—a lot to digest."

Mrs. Quinn reached for Clara's hand across the table and Clara let her take it. "I also have to apologize to you, dear. I was too caught up in my own emotions to consider yours. I know your heart tells you something different from the DNA report as far as who your family is, but in my heart, you're my little girl. Even though you may not want it, at least not yet, I wasn't being a very good mother yesterday."

"You didn't feel relief and happiness. I'm sure it was difficult for you to ring the doorbell and tell your story. None of us took the time to remember that. It's something a mother should know."

"We should *all* have considered your feelings," Mr. Quinn agreed.

"I won't deny that yesterday was a difficult day, but I understood your reaction," Clara said, deciding to be honest and not hide anything. "I don't want you to think that it doesn't affect me to meet you. It does. So much. I just didn't know that I had you to miss."

"Maybe we just need to take things one day at a time. There's no manual for a situation like this, and when it comes to feelings, there are no rights and wrongs. Empathy will get us a long way."

Clara nodded to Mrs. Quinn, relieved that she wasn't as alone as she had been feeling despite always being surrounded by Quinns.

It turned out to be quite a pleasant meal even without her new life buoy, Luke. She thawed a lot in regard to Mr. and Mrs. Quinn. She was hopeful that in time, things would become even easier.

"We have some things for you," Mrs. Quinn said that afternoon. "Over the years, I've thought a lot about what it would be like if...When you came home... As time passed, I realized that if we ever got you back, we wouldn't be getting a baby back, but a girl, then a teenager, then a young woman. Part of me forgot that yesterday, but it's been on my mind a lot since you were taken from us. So I've been making photo albums for you—as a way for you to get a glimpse of what's happened while you've been gone. I hope you'll take them."

She offered Clara three thick, leather-bound albums.

"Wow. Thank you." Clara ran her fingertips over the leather on the top one. "I really appreciate these. I'm not as organized with my pictures...The ones from my parents, too, but I do have them all backed up online. I can have some printed for you if you'd like?"

"Please." Mrs. Quinn's reply was so quick and heartfelt that she laughed at herself. "Sorry. Yes, please. We'd love any pictures you'd like to share with us. Twenty-seven years is such a long time."

Clara nodded and bit the inside of her cheek. Maybe she was seeing things clearer than the previous day, too. Being away from someone you loved for almost thirty years, never knowing if you would see them again… Tears welled up in her eyes and she furiously blinked them away.

"There's also this." Mr. Quinn produced a box about three times the size of a regular shoebox. "It's filled with birthday cards, Christmas cards and drawings from when the kids were younger. Little mementos from over the years. In the beginning, we bought you presents every year for your birthday and Christmas, but as the years passed, we donated the toys and the clothes. There are some presents in here, but not a lot. Instead, you'll see certificates from the charities we've donated money to instead."

"And there's also this." He handed her an envelope. "All your grandparents—your *biological* grandparents—have passed away. They left some things for you in their wills. The things are in the box, and the money was put into an account in your name along with your trust fund, which was released when you turned twenty-one and your college fund. We had one for all our children. The information is in the envelope."

Curling her fingers, Clara pulled her hand back as if the envelope was on fire. "I…I can't tell you what it means to me that I've been a part of your lives all this time, but... The pictures and letters are one thing; I really appreciate them. But I can't take your money."

"It's your money."

She shook her head. Just when she'd thought things were becoming easier. "No, it's not. I don't know how to explain it to you when I can't even explain it to myself. I don't mean to be ungrateful. It just wouldn't feel right to take it."

After a beat, Mrs. Quinn took the envelope and put it on the table. "We can discuss that later."

Although there was no more talk about money, the uneasy feeling stayed with Clara as they asked questions about her life and told her about their own. It didn't help when Duncan showed up and charmed an enormous piece of chocolate cake out of Mrs. Quinn, although she'd already put it away. Then he plopped down on the couch next to Clara and sent her a smile while he inhaled his cake.

Attractive idiot.

"He's got a sixth sense when it comes to cake," Rachel said with a snort and ducked as he reached out to pull her hair.

"It's a highly cultivated skill. Besides, there's no chocolate cake like Mama Q's. It's a fact."

Clara decided to ignore him and turned to ask Mr. Quinn something that had occurred to her that she didn't know. She could have missed it in the private investigator's report, but she wasn't sure it had been in there.

"When is my birthday?"

Even Rachel shut up at her question.

"What do you mean?" Mr. Quinn asked.

"I mean whoever took me and brought me to Denmark probably wouldn't know my birthday. Even if they did, it would make sense to put something else on my fake birth certificate, which says I was born on April twelfth."

"You were born on April twenty-first," he replied quietly.

"One of the happiest days of our lives," Mrs. Quinn added.

Clara swallowed with some difficulty. It was surreal to have a new birthday. "April twenty-first. Right. Thanks."

"If you can get Luke to share the cake," Duncan commented and scowled at Rachel when she elbowed him in the stomach. "What?"

"Seriously," Rachel muttered. "Could you be anymore insensitive?"

"Easily," he shot back. "But I wasn't being insensitive. I was trying to lighten the mood."

Like that morning in the hotel lobby, the sibling—or almost sibling—bickering amused her as well as annoyed her a little. It also made her jealous. Duncan made her want to kick his ass and kiss him senseless at the same time. The attraction clearly hadn't been dimmed by time and distance.

There was another big family dinner to get through. Clara was fairly sure the Quinns didn't do that every night, so that meant that she was the occasion. She longed for peace and quiet, but did her best to keep up with what everyone was talking about. She answered what seemed like a million questions, asked some herself and when it was all over, she felt even more confused than before.

Back at the hotel after dinner, Clara dug in for a quiet night. She needed some time to decompress and whether they wanted to admit it or not, so did the Quinns. Crawling into bed, she leaned her back against the headboard and grabbed one of the toffees she'd bought. Candy was the answer to so many of life's questions. Often it was the wrong answer, but an answer nonetheless. She turned the TV on and found a music channel. Then, she finally picked up the photo albums Mrs. Quinn had given her.

They were numbered, so she started with the first one. She had meant to take a deep breath, but it shuddered right out of her body when she looked at the first page. The caption read 'Eve & Lucas.' Two pink babies lay together on a blanket, holding hands. They were wearing similar rompers, only one was light blue and the other light pink. Her and Luke. Everything suddenly became a lot more real.

On the following pages were more pictures of baby Eve…Or baby Clara. With Luke, with Ben, with Danny, with Mrs. and Mr. Quinn. All proof that she had indeed belonged to the Quinn family once. And they loved their baby Eve. It was clear in every single picture.

Then there were no more pictures of baby Eve. Not as many smiles. The boys grew older; a new baby girl came along, as did an almost black-haired boy who didn't smile much. Clara's heart ached for all of them. For the Quinns, who had lost their Eve and for Duncan, who clearly hadn't been a happy child.

Children became teenagers. Teenagers became adults. Girlfriends and boyfriends, grandparents, wives and then children. It was like a big, woven Quinn quilt, where love was the center motif. There were birthdays and Christmases. Halloweens and Thanksgivings. Graduations, family dinners and vacations.

She once again choked on her breath when she saw pictures of tables set for Christmas, always with an extra setting and a white rose on one of the plates. Luke. It was almost unfathomable how he'd been able to keep the hope alive for so long. They had been separated when they were only five months old—he'd had no memories of her.

Her finger traced the pattern in the leather on the last album. There was no price on them. Although it was still almost unknown, the albums represented an alternative life story that some unknown person had decided she wasn't allowed to experience. Whoever had grabbed her out of that carriage, had turned so many lives around. Now they would have to build everything up using photographs and words.

She looked longingly at the box of letters and other things. She was curious and wanted to explore it, but looking through the albums had shown her how important visuals were. So she needed to return the favor. The next hours were spent looking through the photos she had stored online. She ordered a bunch of them as prints to be delivered to the Quinn house. The rest she would burn onto a blank CD as soon as she could get her hands on one.

By the time that was done, she was too tired to look at the box. She turned off the TV and the lights, cocooning herself under the covers.

She fell asleep thinking about Duncan. It had been easier to suppress the memories of him at home when she had believed she'd never see him again. Seeing him once more brought everything back to the surface—the romance, the laughter and their amazing nights together. How much it had hurt not hearing from him. How difficult it had been to get over what had turned out to be no more than a vacation fling.

The last thing she remembered before sleep took her was cursing him to hell and back for making everything more difficult.

Chapter Four

Duncan was not unfamiliar with the feeling of having his life bombed into atoms and then having to pick up the pieces to see if he could get them to fit somehow. He'd tried it as a kid when his dad had gone from punching him once in a while to beating the ever-loving shit out of him. Instead of taking him to see a doctor, his mom had opened a bottle of wine. Unlucky for her and lucky for him, Grace Quinn had stopped by with the raincoat he'd forgotten at the Quinn house. His mom had unthinkingly opened the door, and Grace had spotted him lying at the bottom of the stairs in a heap. The Quinns had offered him a new life but a lot of it he'd been forced to piece together himself inside his head.

Meeting Clara in Bali had changed his life again. He remembered the disappointment vividly when he'd called the number she'd given him the first time. And the second. And the third. It had been so brief, only a few days and nights together, but he'd felt something that he'd wanted to explore more. It had been hard work to accept that it wouldn't happen, but he'd done it.

Then she'd appeared in his path again—as Eve Quinn of all people.

He hammered in the last nail with a lot more effort than required and leaned back on his heels to inspect his work. He'd never admitted to anyone why he'd bought an old house that needed years of work and love. It was his therapy. He didn't want counseling or sleeping pills. He wanted to exhaust himself every night by replacing windows, stripping floors and figuring out wiring. He wanted to be so busy that he wouldn't think of a dark-haired beauty with a sinful body, and he wanted to be so exhausted that he fell into dreamless sleep, never even remembering that the word 'insomnia' existed. He wanted something to distract him from how much a brief encounter with a stranger had messed him up.

The window seat he'd added to the small sitting room next to the master bedroom looked nice. It was everything he'd imagined it to be in his head, minus the woman sitting there, reading a book. He didn't even know if Clara liked to read.

As he packed up his tools and cleaned up, he thought about her. There was nothing unusual in that, but he tried to imagine what she was going through at the moment. The part of him who wanted to lay into her for her shitty handwriting and then seduce her back into bed had too much respect for the turmoil she was facing with a new, unknown family, who expected her to be a five-month-old baby called Eve. There was something inside of him that ached for her, felt her pain and confusion. Yet he had no idea what he could do to make it easier for her.

When he fell asleep half an hour later, she was still on his mind, sneaking into a not so innocent dream.

The next morning, Duncan didn't feel fully awake until he stepped into the coffee shop. He loved the smell and greedily drank it in. He didn't even mind waiting in line just because it meant he could soak in the smell before actually drinking the brew.

When he stepped into his studio a little later with four cups of coffee in a cup holder, he felt ready to face the day.

"Morning, guys."

"Good morning, boss." Emily looked up from whatever she was doing and smiled. Peter grunted something but didn't look away from the computer screen. He had a rocky relationship with computers and preferred his old cameras and the darkroom. Duncan knew he'd hit the jackpot with his employees. He never had to worry when he decided to take an assignment out of town. The studio was in capable hands with Emily and Peter.

"Your first appointment cancelled," Emily told him, giving him a handwritten message. "Kid got the chickenpox."

"Poor kid." Duncan crumbled the note and threw it away. He remembered the chickenpox. He and the Quinn kids had shared that horrendous experience, and he was the only one with scars. Damn Quinns and their willpower.

He went into his office with two of the coffees. Even though he'd bought the extra cup, he was still a little surprised to see that the office wasn't empty with everything that was happening. "Good morning, Papa Q. You're early today."

"Morning, son. Grace threw me out."

Duncan dumped himself in a chair with raised eyebrows.

"I just grabbed a couple of the cinnamon rolls she'd made. How was I supposed to know they were for someone else?"

Sliding the coffee across the table, Duncan laughed. "You probably took more than a couple."

"Five." Carl Quinn grinned. "One to eat on the way here and two for each of us."

"I'll put in a good word for you since you're sharing the goods." The pastries were a plus, but Duncan treasured the mornings with the man he considered his father. After he'd stopped working full days, he'd been... Well, *bored* was probably not the right word. Restless maybe. Papa Q had worked hard all his life, dedicated to his job, his family and to the continued search for his daughter.

So with more time on his hands, he'd started dropping in almost every morning for a cup of coffee and a chat before Duncan started his workday. Often, he'd then wander over to Luke's shop for a while before putting in a few hours of work himself.

"I appreciate it."

"So, how are you and Mama Q doing?" That first night, Duncan had mostly observed as the Quinns had drowned Clara in questions, hugs and teary-eyed declarations. Not that he could blame them, but it was like he'd been an outsider enough to see things a little from Clara's perspective, too. No one else had, as far as he could see. He'd also been caught up in his own thoughts about her.

"Having Eve back feels like the answer to every prayer I've ever said." The joy and elation was visible on the older man's face. "You hope and you dream. Sometimes you tell yourself to be realistic. Other times, you despair. It's been almost three decades of ups and downs as far as hoping. Besides being over-the-moon happy, I also feel weird. I barely know myself as a man *without* a missing daughter. It's been part of my identity for so long."

Duncan nodded thoughtfully and sipped his coffee as he continued to listen to a man who clearly had something he needed to get off his chest.

"There are a lot of emotions to deal with. I'm bitter that someone else got to raise my daughter and see her grow, but I'm grateful that they were good to her and that she's alive. I'm frustrated that they turned our Eve into their Clara. I'm proud of what an amazing young woman she appears to be. I'm scared that she'll somehow disappear again one day. I… It's all muddled up inside of me."

"A tiny detail you'd overlooked when dreaming about her return?" Duncan asked.

Carl laughed and nodded before sighing tiredly. "Definitely."

"From what I could tell when I talked to her yesterday morning, she's as confused by her emotions as you are. Who can blame any of you? It's probably just going to take time."

"I hope so. Now I'll get out of your hair. I'm sure you have people to photograph."

"In about twenty minutes, yeah."

"You work too much, son. The camera at day and the house at night."

Duncan smiled. It was a familiar tune by now. "The house is almost done, you know that. Just a few finishing touches left. I completed the window seat in the room next to the master bedroom last night."

"You don't read that many books."

"I might start. How else am I going to spend all that free time I'll have on my hands once there's no more to do at the house?"

"You'll find something." Carl grinned. "Take care of yourself."

"You too. And tell Mama Q the cinnamon roll theft was just a good deed. I hadn't had breakfast. There's no way she can resist that."

The rolls turned out to be his lunch, too, as he skipped his lunch break to deal with someone dropping in without an appointment. It was such a busy day that he had little time to think about Clara—except when he had a second to spare and he wondered what she might be doing. He discovered, not for the first time, that he often had a second to spare for Clara even when he was busy.

He was busy until it was time to leave for the day. Instead of heading home, he went directly to Vanessa and Ben's house. If he knew Vanessa, there would be something delicious cooking on the stove or in the oven for him and the kids. He was babysitting Tommy and Leanne while Vanessa and Ben went to some charity thing. He hadn't really been paying attention when they'd told him what it was. He just loved spending time with the kids, and the kids loved their Uncle Dunc best, a fact that he never got tired of rubbing in Luke, Danny, or Rachel's faces. Of course, Rachel claimed it was because he was a kid himself. But she was just jealous.

"Uncle Dunc!" Tommy came running as soon as he stepped into the house.

"Hey, buddy." He swung the wildly giggling boy into the air before giving him a hug.

"Uncle Dunc, I drewed you a picture of my new aunty. Wanna see?"

"I'd love to. I bet it's beautiful." What else could it be when it was a drawing of Clara made by the smartest four-year-old in the world?

Tommy ran off to find his drawing as Vanessa came out with Leanne on her hip. The little girl instantly reached for Duncan, who grabbed her with a laugh.

"All the pretty girls want me."

"Hey, Duncan. Thanks for doing this." Vanessa kissed him on the cheek and put on an earring.

"Anytime." Leanne had attached her sticky mouth to his cheek and he laughed, jiggling her.

"Sorry about that." Vanessa produced a Kleenex.

"You don't wipe off a girl's kisses. It's not polite." Duncan followed the smell of something delicious to the kitchen. "What's for dinner?"

Vanessa followed. "Let me guess. No lunch?"

"Didn't have time."

"Duncan…" She sighed. "There's a casserole in the oven."

"I love you." He put Leanne in her high chair just as Tommy came running in. The boy rarely walked anywhere. "You kids hungry?"

"Uncle Dunc, you have to see my picture!"

Duncan sat down and let Tommy climb onto his lap. "Let's see your masterpiece."

"See? It's my new aunty. I think she's real pretty." Tommy put the drawing on the table.

"Yes, she is." Duncan nearly snorted at the understatement. The

31

drawing had a Picasso-like resemblance to Clara, at least if you were an adoring uncle, who thought your nephew was a genius. "That is an awesome drawing, buddy. Maybe you'll be an artist like your new aunty."

"Daddy says she draws pictures."

"He's right."

Tommy considered this for a moment, his face all scrunched up. "Do you think she's better than me?"

"What? Of course not! I only hang the best drawings on my fridge and they're all yours, aren't they?"

Pleased, Tommy nodded and hopped down. "Yep. You can have this one to hang on your fridge, too, Uncle Dunc."

"Thank you very much." He ruffled the boy's hair.

Somewhere in the house, he heard Vanessa yelling at Ben that they were late. After the usual instructions that he could recite in his sleep, Ben and Vanessa left. Duncan decided it was dinnertime.

Tommy talked all through the meal and Leanne got mashed potatoes in her hair. It was the best dinner Duncan had had in weeks. Bath time was a challenge as Leanne was going through an 'I don't like water' phase. Duncan sang to her to distract her while Tommy flooded the bathroom floor. Then he had to clean up while both kids took off the pajamas he'd just gotten them into and hid under Tommy's bed.

The whole thing made him smile. It reminded him of his childhood after he'd moved in with the Quinns. Despite the underlying sadness, it had always been a happy and safe home. Vanessa and Ben had created the same for their kids.

"Tell a story, Uncle Dunc," Tommy sleepily begged when he and Leanne were dressed again and tucked into their beds.

So he did. One about a dragon—Tommy vetoed the princess—who got lost and then took a long time finding its way home.

It was nice to be able to collapse on the couch when the house was finally quiet. It was fun to deal with the kids, but it was also more exhausting than sanding floors or fixing the roof. He didn't bother turning the TV on. Instead, he dug out his cell phone and scrolled down to find Gertrud's number. It had been a while since he'd talked to her, but then he remembered the time difference. It was too late in Denmark to call her now. He wanted to hear how she was doing and tell her that he'd finally found his girl again.

It was a strange thing that he'd formed a friendship with an old woman across the world because of Clara's crappy handwriting. He'd truly believed that she'd done it on purpose after finally realizing that Gertrud didn't know Clara. But she hadn't. That fact had almost drowned in the whole Clara being Eve business. He was relieved. Although their time together in Bali had been short, it had changed him.

He sat up when an idea hit him. On his phone, he found a website where he could order flowers and have them delivered in Denmark. He had Gertrud's phone number; the rest of her information would be easy to dig up. Making people smile wasn't difficult, but sometimes it seemed like it was a forgotten art.

Duncan fell asleep at some point and didn't wake up until Ben threw a cushion on his face. Older brothers were nice like that. He sat up, rubbing his eyes. "Vanessa, why do you put up with that idiot when you could run away with me? I don't go around throwing things at sleeping people."

She laughed and kicked off her heels before plopping down on the couch next to him. "Beats me. Maybe I love him?"

"In that case, you deserve him. Did you have a good time?"

"It was okay. Only Ben's mind was a million miles away the whole time." She nodded toward her husband. "Like now. He has no idea we're even here. I could tell you that I'm pregnant and he wouldn't react."

Duncan looked at Ben and then back at Vanessa. "Are you?"

"No. But he'd freak if I were. I think it's the 'Eve Syndrome.'"

Yawning, Duncan threw the cushion back at Ben, who was standing by the fireplace, staring at nothing. "I think most of the family caught that."

"What?" Ben looked confused.

"Nothing. Just checking to see if you're still awake."

"I was just thinking…"

"About Clara?" Duncan stood up and stretched. Looking at his watch, he saw that it was past eleven.

"Yeah," Ben replied, loosening his tie. "I can't wrap my mind around it, you know?"

"I think that's going around. Give it time."

Ben hummed in agreement, but seemed lost in his own thoughts again.

"I suppose we can't blame him—or any of them," Duncan said to Vanessa. "They remember baby Eve and get a fully grown Clara twenty-seven years later."

"Mind-blowing," she agreed. "Thanks for watching the kids tonight, Duncan. I hope they weren't too much trouble."

"It was fun. You know I love them."

"That's your way of saying that they *were* trouble. I'm sorry." She squeezed his arm as she passed by him. "Hang on, let me apologize with the leftovers."

"You're right. They were little devils. Leftovers are the only cure for my traumatized state."

Laughing, she sweetened the pot with banana bread and a little later, he left. His bed was calling his name across town.

Chapter Five

Clara woke up to a buzzing cell phone. She blindly reached for it and wondered what time it was. It seemed awfully early if the dark room was anything to go by. "Hello?" she managed through a yawn.

"Good morning, sunshine. Are you up yet?"

"Define up."

Luke laughed. "Sorry if I woke you. I rearranged some stuff and now have the day off. I was hoping I could spend it with you."

Opening her eyes, Clara reached for the light switch so she could see her wristwatch. Barely after seven. "Do you call everyone this early?"

"Only when I want something."

"Well, I'm awake anyway. Buy me something warm and sweet for breakfast and you're on."

Half an hour later, Clara was drinking piping hot coffee and eating a still-warm apple Danish while Luke drove them out of town. She'd wait until she finished her coffee to wonder where they were going. For now, she just needed to wake up.

"Are those things really Danish?"

"Huh?" She looked over at him.

"The Danishes."

She looked at the pastry. "We have them in Denmark, but we call them Vienna bread."

"For real? That's weird."

Clara shrugged and sipped her coffee. Stranger things *had* happened in her life. Getting a twenty-seven-year-old twin out of the blue was just one example.

"You seem very relaxed today," he commented. "Or are you still asleep?"

"Both," she offered honestly. "All of you at the same time... It's intimidating. It's easier to relax when it's just you. It's so weird because it feels like I know you."

"I think you do. Not a lot of people believe this, but I feel like I've always known you. I've developed a theory over the years, and you're the only one who can confirm it."

"Sounds interesting." She drained her coffee cup and looked at him expectantly.

He chuckled, but it was endearing how he looked a little nervous. "I wasn't very old when I heard myself being called moody for the first time. Sometimes, I'd start crying out of the blue. Or laugh loudly. It appeared random to Mom and Dad and the people in school. Ben and Danny gave me hell about it for years, calling me a sissy. But I felt it, you know? Sometimes pain would hit me out of nowhere, like I'd fallen or banged my head against something. Or I'd feel laughter bubbling up in my throat. I know people thought—well, they probably still think it, although I've gotten better at hiding it—that I was crazy. But I think it was you that I could feel."

Clara wanted to dismiss it because it did, indeed, sound crazy. But she couldn't. It didn't just sound crazy, it also sounded familiar. When she didn't say anything, Luke continued.

"I think I was around fourteen when I started writing the stuff down, hoping that one day I could show you. It was why I never lost hope that you were alive, even when people kept telling us that you'd probably died as a baby." He turned to look at her. "Have you ever felt anything you couldn't explain? I mean, I realize you couldn't pin it on a twin since you didn't know I existed, but maybe just something you thought was strange or weird?"

"Well…" She hesitated briefly. "Like you said, I didn't have an explanation, but maybe there have been some things. Don't laugh, but I was well into my teens before I got rid of my imaginary friend, Balder."

Luke didn't laugh. "What was Balder like?"

It was strange to talk to someone about such a private thing. "He was… Always there, like a best friend who never had to go home for dinner. I don't know—it's difficult to explain. I guess you could say he was a comfort."

"I'm glad you had him. I suppose in some ways you were *my*

imaginary friend."

Clara blew out a breath and stared out the window at the passing landscape. "It's weird to talk about, but it makes sense somehow."

"We don't have to talk about it anymore, but I do have a journal I'd like you to read. Just things I've felt that didn't make sense, which I think have been you. Maybe you could be the one to tell me I'm not crazy."

She looked at him. He was staring straight ahead with his jaw tightly set. "I'd love to read it, but you don't strike me as the crazy type. It doesn't matter what people say or think. If you felt it, then it was there."

His short laugh was strained. "God, I wish you'd been around all these years."

Clara didn't agree, not fully anyway. Agreeing would be the same as saying that she would have rather been without her wonderful childhood in Denmark. She also couldn't disagree as that meant stomping all over Luke's feelings. As far as he was concerned, then she did wish they'd had each other all along. Maybe it was the special bond between twins, maybe it was just that they clicked as human beings but so far, Luke was her favorite Quinn. By Quinns, she also meant the thorn in her side called Duncan Cantwell.

"Where are we going?" she asked, purposely changing the subject.

It had the desired effect as Luke smiled. "Antique market up north, which means I may sneak in a little work, but mainly because I thought you'd enjoy it. They've got lots of art."

Clara straightened in the seat. "Why didn't you say so? I wouldn't even have needed coffee to wake up if I'd known."

Luke laughed. "That's nice. My company isn't enough. Old paintings, however..."

"A girl's gotta have her priorities."

Smiling as he looked straight on, he shook his head. "Sometimes it's scary how much you and Rachel are alike."

"Really?" For some reason, it made her smile.

They had a great time at the antique market. Clara wandered off on her own while Luke handled some stuff for his store and later, she offered her opinion on some paintings he considered buying.

Looking at the artwork, she realized that she missed painting. She hadn't touched a paintbrush since that night she'd gotten the first indication that her life was a lie. Inspiration had simply eluded her. Just getting through the classes she taught had been a nightmare.

"You're everywhere, aren't you?"

Clara jumped and turned to see a grinning Duncan. "No, I tend to stick to one place at a time."

"Touché. What are you doing here?"

"Mowing my front lawn."

He rolled his eyes. "Has anyone ever told you that you're a lot more attractive when you're being nice?"

"Has anyone ever told you that you're an idiot?"

"Mature," he commented. "Really mature."

"Like you're one to speak." Clara was relieved to see Luke walk up to them.

"Hey, Dunc. Finding anything good?"

"A bit," Duncan replied, holding up some frames. "You didn't tell me you were heading up here today."

"Sorry, last minute thing. I wanted to show this place to Clara. I was looking for frames, though. Got you a couple that are being packed with my stuff."

"Thanks, man."

"Anytime." Luke turned to Clara. "Duncan often tags along to look for frames for his studio. People like that they can buy vintage ones with their photographs."

"That's a really good idea," she told Duncan, trying to be civil. Not that it was easy when she wanted to smack him and kiss him at the same time whenever she saw him.

He smirked. "Why, thank you."

As she glared at him, she felt Luke looking at her. Then at Duncan. "What is it with you two?"

"What do you mean?" Clara dug out the acting skills she hadn't used since fifth grade and a poor version of Mozart's *The Magic Flute*.

The way Luke narrowed his eyes at her made her giggle. He looked like such a *brother* and it was exhilarating.

"Remember the girl from Bali a few years ago that I told you about?" Duncan interrupted, directing his question at Luke.

"The one who gave you a fake phone number? What was her name again?"

Clara gasped. He hadn't actually told Luke, had he? The grin Duncan sent her was lethal, and she wanted to poke her tongue at him. Yes, she was *so* mature.

"Yep. It was Clara. Our Clara."

"Dude! No way." Luke looked at her, wide-eyed. Duncan was still grinning.

"The phone number wasn't fake!" was the only thing she could think of to say.

"No, it was just wrong." Duncan pulled out his wallet and produced the receipt she'd hurriedly written her phone number on more than two years earlier.

She couldn't believe he'd kept it. It was so sweet. At that moment, she wanted to kiss him more than she wanted to slap him, but it didn't last long.

He shoved it under her nose. "See? That's clearly an eight, not a three."

Snatching the scrap of paper, she looked at it. It wasn't an eight. She had without a shadow of doubt, written it as a three. What was just as clear to her was that it did look like an eight. She's been in a rush to catch her flight, and Marie was right when she'd said that her handwriting lacked elegance when she wrote fast. There was no way she was about to admit it to Duncan.

"It's a three. I know my own phone number."

Luke reached for the receipt. "I already looked at this—as did Danny, Rachel, Ben, Vanessa and Linda—and we all agreed it was an eight. It's one of the few times we've all agreed on something over Sunday brunch."

Clara closed her eyes. Of course, it had to be at Sunday brunch that Duncan had shared his vacation memories. Could it get any more embarrassing?

"Now that I think about it, I think Dad wanted it to be a three, but we outnumbered him," Luke said.

Apparently, it could. Mr. Quinn had seen it, too and no doubt heard whatever version of the story Duncan had shared with them. God, she hoped he'd left out the details. *All* the details.

"Remind me, always to listen to Papa Q in the future." Duncan took the receipt from Luke and put it back in his wallet. The look he sent her was impossible for her to read.

"Why didn't you say anything the first day? I mean, you must have recognized each other." Luke looked between them.

"It wasn't really the time or the place," Duncan replied. He was looking at Clara, but she refused to meet his gaze.

She'd preferred that they'd worked things out in private instead of involving others. Part of her was extremely embarrassed. Apart from Marie, she wasn't in the habit of sharing personal issues with anyone. Of course, she didn't know how sibling bonds worked—or kind of sibling bonds. She also didn't really know if Luke and Duncan were just best friends. She didn't know anything except that she was uncomfortable and needed air. She was suffocating.

"Excuse me," she said and nearly ran toward the closest exit.

There were almost as many people outside as inside, but at least there was fresh air. She berated herself for letting things get to her while she paced back and forth. In the past year, she'd gone days without thinking about Duncan, but now that he was around all the time, he got to her. She didn't want to admit her mistake with the rushed phone number. She didn't understand his behavior. And she couldn't get him out of her head. Memories, new and old, floated around in there constantly, often mixed up with dreams of what she'd like to do to him. Violently or passionately.

"Hey, you okay?"

Again, she jumped as he'd snuck up on her without her noticing. She didn't know where Luke was, but Duncan was alone.

"I'm fine. I just needed air."

"You didn't want me to tell Luke."

It wasn't a question, but she wanted to answer anyway. "No. I thought we should have worked it out alone. It's difficult enough... With the Quinns."

"I'm sorry. The last thing I want is make things harder for you. But it happened, Clara, and I don't hide shit for no reason."

She sighed. "You don't hide shit for no reason? Wow, where was that expression in my high school English book?"

Duncan grinned. She hated that grin. And loved it. It made her tingle in places she had no business tingling for him anymore. "Listen, baby. No one is going to care what happened between us in Bali. Sure, there will be the 'if only' crap that Danny tortures himself with, but let's be honest. There's no way I could have known who you were."

"I know that! I do. It's just... I don't know. I'm not used to having a family where you share things like that." She rubbed her temples, willing the approaching headache away without success. "Maybe I should have said 'hey, that's the guy I met in Bali!' when Mr. Quinn showed me that family portrait, but I didn't."

"It doesn't matter."

She stared at him. "What?"

"We can talk about it from now until Christmas. It won't change anything."

"Right." Clara felt defeated all of the sudden and she wasn't entirely sure why.

"Let's go back inside and find Luke before he buys the whole place," Duncan said and walked ahead of her back inside the market.

Clara followed. She fought the ever-present tears by shooting daggers at Duncan's back. It helped a lot.

Once they'd found Luke, Duncan left them. Clara tried to act as if she was okay, even if she felt anything but. Luke, wisely, didn't comment on what he'd just learned. Instead, they discussed art and managed to find some great pieces for his shop. Clara was tempted to buy a large painting of a red oak with the most amazing detail, but just the thought of how to get it shipped to Denmark without damaging it, made her let Luke buy it instead.

When they drove back south toward Stonebridge, the ease between them was back. They traded childhood stories. Luke's were funnier than hers, especially because of the antics he and his brothers had been up to. Often, Rachel had been on the receiving end of their pranks, but Clara enjoyed hearing about their punishments when Mrs. Quinn found out, too. Boys teasing girls deserved to get an extra serving of green beans instead of dessert. It did make her wish she'd been there, just so she could have helped Rachel stand up to the bully boys. Her heart softened when Luke then shared stories of how protective, bordering on overprotective, they'd always been of Rachel.

"She'd probably never gone anywhere on her own before she went away for college," he told Clara. "Even though it's close, we all hate it that we can't be there for her. I think she enjoys it, though she always understood why we acted like we did. Losing one sister was enough."

The guilt filled her even though it wasn't her fault that her disappearance had such impact on her siblings' life. But whoever was at fault, it was still difficult to bear.

Clara ordered room service for dinner that night. She wasn't in the mood to be social. The Quinns would just have to deal with the fact that she needed alone time once in a while. She wasn't used to a big family and people around all the time.

After she'd eaten, she dug into the box Mr. Quinn had given her. She looked at childish drawings done by her siblings, getting a little teary-eyed at how many of them portrayed the Quinn family with her present. There were birthday cards, some of them from grandparents she'd never gotten a chance to know. They all expressed hope that she'd be there with them on the next birthday. There were also birthday cards from Duncan, which was a little weird. Although, she supposed it wasn't any weirder than the ones from Rachel. None of them had known baby Eve. The cards from Duncan included from an impressively early age, the most charming snapshots of everything and everyone. Clara collected them in a pile, determined to give them the frame or album they deserved.

Small boxes held what appeared to be heirloom jewelry. There was an old journal from a Josephine Quinn, who Clara gathered was Mr. Quinn's mother. So many little notes of love, grief and frustration. Dried, white roses pressed in a notebook. The tears came without her even noticing at first. It was a box full of history, a history of love and grief, hope and frustration.

Chapter Six

Clara had been invited to Sunday brunch at Vanessa and Ben's house. The Quinns were all there, as well as some of Vanessa's family. It was total chaos, with children running around and people talking and laughing. Not without charm, but overwhelming for the only child of only-child parents.

Standing by herself for a precious moment, she watched Duncan snap photos of the kids playing. They barely even noticed him and when they did, he just laughed and said something silly.

It was the photography that had caught Clara's attention in Bali initially. He had been taking pictures of children then, too—young boys and girls fishing from rocks on the beach. He moved with such ease, snapping photo after photo. Photography interested her, but it hadn't taken long for the photographer to become more interesting than his art.

Back then, he'd already had his own studio but enjoyed taking the occasional job for a magazine somewhere exotic. She didn't know if he still did that, but he hadn't lost any of his magic. They had walked and talked on the beach, embarrassingly she had even posed for him. Nothing shady, just a happy, laughing, young woman with flowers in her hair. They'd gone sightseeing, although Clara didn't remember what they'd seen. They'd laughed, danced and spent the most amazing nights in his hotel room, exploring each other to the sound of their staccato breaths and the waves crashing against the shore outside the open windows. It had been perfect. Then, he hadn't called because he claimed she couldn't write down her own phone number.

Her cell phone vibrated and shook her from the memories. She stepped out on the chilly back porch to answer it. It was her friend, Marie, and it was like slipping into a worn and comfortable pair of shoes when she switched back to her own language.

"Why haven't you called me? I've been going out of my mind wondering how you're doing. Who knew if your new family had chained you up in the basement?"

"Sorry." Clara shook her head in amusement. "They're much nicer than that, luckily. But you were the one who was so against me going. It hurt when you said I was dishonoring my parents' memory, Marie."

"I know. I'm sorry, sweetie. I wasn't thinking. Forgive me?"

Marie was scatterbrained, generous with her not always thought-through opinions, but she was loyal when it mattered. She was also her best friend, although she'd made the terrible decision of moving across the country so they rarely saw each other anymore.

"Forgiven."

"Thanks. Now, tell me everything."

Clara laughed. "Considering how expensive this call is, I'll save the whole story for another time. But I met them, my biological parents. They're really nice. I'm just overwhelmed with everything. I've got three brothers and a sister. Can you believe it? I even have an honest-to-God twin! My mind can't wrap itself around all that."

"Wow. Some people get a baby brother and you get three brothers at once. And a sister. Nice going. I'm really glad that your parents are nice. That's the most important thing, right?"

"Yeah. And guess what? The guy I met in Bali?"

"Mr. Hunky Photographer. Yes, I remember the moping when he never called."

"He's like the half-adopted kid of the family. They treat him like a son and a brother."

"Dude! What did he say when he saw you?"

"Not much. Later, he told me that he hadn't called because I wrote down the wrong phone number. As if."

"Easy cop out. Although, your handwriting does suck when you're in a rush."

"It does not!"

"Oh, it does, sweetie. Half the time I can't make sense of your notes, and I'm used to them."

"Fine. Take his side."

Marie laughed delightedly. "I'm not taking his side. Why would I?

He's the asshole who didn't call you. I'm just stating facts."

"I don't like your facts. I know how to write." Clara pouted for good measure and turned when she heard the glass door slide open. It was Ben, who mouthed 'sorry' and started to retreat when he saw that she was on the phone. She smiled at him and shook her head, motioning him outside. It was his back porch, after all.

"I gotta go," she told Marie in Danish. "I really appreciate your call, and maybe we can Skype one night so I can tell you everything?"

"That's a date. Take care of yourself, Clara."

"You, too. Bye."

With a relieved smile that at least some things were as they had always been, she pocketed the phone and turned to Ben. "Sorry. Friend back in Denmark wanting to make sure I hadn't been chained up in the Quinn basement."

He chuckled. "No chains down there, just the occasional spider. I'm sorry, I didn't mean to interrupt. I just saw you out here and wanted to make sure you were okay."

"I'm fine, thanks."

"Good." He stood awkwardly looking like he was torn between wanting to stay and wanting to leave. Clara knew the feeling, but she hated that she brought it out in him. Usually, it took more than just a single Quinn to make her feel that way.

"Do you often have big family brunches like this?" Clara asked when she couldn't handle the uncomfortable silence any longer. She didn't know why Ben was so tense and in turn, making her just as tense.

"What? Oh. Yeah, at least once a month we try to get everyone together. It's hard sometimes, though. People are busy..." He ran his hand through his short hair. "Listen, I've been trying to catch you alone. I need to apologize to you."

"Apologize? Whatever for?"

He emitted a sound that might have been called a laugh if there had been any joy in it. But there wasn't. "Two things, actually. This is going to sound..."

"If it helps, I can't think of a single thing you could possibly want to apologize for. We barely even know each other."

"I know and that's part of it. The day you were taken, you and Luke were napping in the carriage on the back porch. Danny was napping in his room. Mom was cooking. She was just starting her catering business back then. I was playing out back while waiting for Danny to wake up. I heard the car, Clara, and I saw a woman coming up to the house. I was supposed to keep an eye on you and Luke… Get Mom if I heard you cry. You know what I did instead of keeping an eye on you? I went inside to see if Danny was awake because I was bored playing alone—so that woman was free to take you."

He sank down on a deck chair and hid his face in his hands. Clara's heart broke for him so she kneeled down next to him. "Ben, for heaven's sake. You were only what, four years old? I can't imagine anyone blaming you."

"They didn't," he replied without looking up. "But I knew it was my fault. To make it worse, I started wishing you'd never come back. I was convinced that you'd just hate me if you did, so it was better if you stayed away. God help me, I even wished you dead sometimes just so you wouldn't come back one day and make everyone hate me. Some brother I was, huh?"

"Ben? Look at me, please."

It was a wary face that appeared from its hiding place.

She smiled at him. "There is nothing to forgive, but if it makes a difference, then you're officially forgiven. I'm actually glad you went inside for Danny that day. If someone has the conscience to kidnap a child, then they probably also have the conscience to hurt one. If you had been in that woman's way, she might have hurt you. I'm glad she didn't have the chance."

Reaching out for his hand, she gave it a squeeze. "As for hoping I wouldn't come back—you were a child when you thought that, right?"

"Yes, of course. I actually considered joining the police just so I could look for you, but an old knee injury made me unable to meet the physical requirements."

"Well, then. Kids think the strangest things. I once wished my grandmother dead so I wouldn't have to spend every Sunday visiting her two hours away. I hated driving because it used to make me carsick. So you're not alone in that department."

Again, she heard the laugh that wasn't quite a laugh.

"I really hate that you've been carrying all that around all these years," she said. "I wish I could say something to make it better. As it is, I'm having a hard enough time figuring out how all this makes me feel. Part of me aches for your family and the many years of grief and uncertainty. Another part of me knows that if it hadn't happened, a wonderful couple in Denmark would have been deprived of the child they wanted so desperately."

Sighing, she glanced over her shoulder as she heard a roar of laughter from inside. "We can't help what we feel. I understand the little boy who was afraid his family would hate him better than I understand myself at the moment."

"It's not easy for you right now, is it?"

"No. I keep trying to find the right thing to feel. I'm not sure there is such a thing. At the same time, I'm so incredibly fortunate to have found the family I was taken away from as a baby, to ease some of their pain."

"For what it's worth, I can't really describe how happy I am that you found your way back to us. Guilt aside and all that."

"Thank you. I appreciate that. Try to let go of the guilt."

"I'll try." The smile on his face was a typical Quinn smile that she'd seen on several other faces. It made her smile back. Perhaps there was a real brother hidden in Benjamin Quinn.

Another week passed, and Clara got to know the Quinns better. She had dinner with Linda and Danny, helped Mrs. Quinn make cupcakes, went to the movies with Rachel, tried to avoid Duncan and all the things he made her feel. Boy did she feel. But the one she felt most comfortable with was still Luke. It was like a male version of her best friend, only better somehow. Luke picked up on her mood so fast and she had him pegged just as easily. They were so in tune with each other that Rachel decided to write a paper on twin connections for one of her classes.

Clara's days were full of Quinns one way or the other, but it was all wearing on her. All she did was try to cram information into her head all the time, as everyone had memories to share and she had no outlet like she'd had in the past when she'd used her art. It was her way of breathing when things became too much. And things were too much. She didn't know how to say stop without offending or hurting them.

Luke understood her to a certain degree, and she'd spent a couple of nights with him just watching a movie or discussing art. To her great surprise, it was Duncan who dragged her out of her state of semi-gloom and guilt over not feeling the same kind of excitement as the Quinns. He showed up one late afternoon when she'd just crawled into bed for a nap, hoping it would make her insistent headache go away.

"Do you have any idea how beautiful you are?" he greeted her when she opened the door.

She stared, wondering if maybe she had fallen asleep and was dreaming.

Then he brushed past her into the room and looked around. "Where is your jacket?"

"I don't think it will fit you."

He chuckled. "Thanks, but I already have my own. I was thinking more along the lines of letting you wear it, actually."

"Why?" Her hand was still on the door handle, unsure of his purpose and of the effect he had on her.

"Because it's cold outside, and I don't want you to get sick."

"I'm not going out, so that solves the problem."

He took two steps forward until they were so close that he was invading her personal space. She would have taken a step back, but she was backed up against the door. "Can you do me a favor?"

She didn't want to, afraid it was something that would mess up her head and her heart even further but the 'yes' was out of her mouth before she realized it.

"Please, stop fighting me all the time. Just for tonight." Her raised eyebrows made him laugh. "I'm just getting you out of this damn hotel room for a while and cooking you dinner. That's all. Scout's honor."

"You used that expression, 'scout's honor', in Bali, too. And then you admitted you'd never been a boy scout."

"Crap. You remembered that. Well, there's still a home-cooked dinner in it for you plus a chance to see my house. How can you refuse that?"

Clara was amazed how he could go from annoying asshole to adorable in just a few minutes. She tried to suppress her smile. "I was going to take a nap to get rid of my headache."

"Why didn't you say so? I'll throw in a massage guaranteed to make you forget what a headache is."

"Duncan..." She sighed.

"Sit down. I've got magic fingers."

Choking on her breath, she stubbornly remained standing. When she'd caught her breath, she narrowed her eyes at him. "I remember your magic fingers, thank you very much. Why don't we just stick with dinner this time, huh?"

Chuckling, he picked up her jacket from the back of a chair. "Whatever you want."

It was no difficult feat to conjure up images of whatever she wanted. With him. They were quickly banished from her mind, though. If she let him, he could burn her again. It would be the easiest thing in the world to let go, just a second of less than complete self-control and she'd be in over her head, if she weren't already.

Still, minutes later, she found herself in the passenger seat of his car on the way to his house. She knew he lived on the outskirts of town in what she'd heard Danny describe as a 'money-eating box of kindle wood.'

"I have ulterior motives for cooking you dinner tonight," Duncan told her during the drive.

"I'm not the least bit surprised." Clara looked at his grinning profile—his very handsome, grinning profile.

"You see, my birthday is coming up on Friday, and I'm having the family over for dinner. And Aunt Tilda—you haven't met her yet, but have you heard of her?"

"The name sounds familiar. I kind of assumed she had passed away because she hasn't been around."

"Oh no, Mathilda Quinn is very much alive. She's Papa Q's aunt, close to ninety, I think. She's...eccentric. That's putting it mildly. She likes taking cruises, which is why you haven't met her yet. I've been told that when you were taken, she was on one of her cruises, Papa Q contacted her. She supposedly asked him if you were dead. He told her he didn't know, but that they were all praying you weren't. Then she read him the riot act about losing faith. Long story short, we don't contact Aunt Tilda on her cruises unless someone is dead. Though, I know that Papa Q considered contacting her when you came back."

"Sounds like an interesting lady." Clara couldn't quite make up her mind if that was a good or bad thing.

"She is. I adore her in small doses. Anyway, she's coming home on Thursday. Between her and Mama Q, I gotta cook to impress, you know? The thing is; I can cook *almost* as well as Mama Q if you want my unbiased opinion, but baking—complete disaster. And what's a birthday without a cake?"

"Still a birthday?" Clara was amused.

The look Duncan sent her was not amused. "Will you help me bake a cake? Please?"

She laughed. "That's it, the magic word. Sure, I'll help your helpless male self out."

"Don't hold back on the compliments, baby."

Staring into the twilight as they turned away from the main road, she briefly wondered if he was taking her into the woods to kill her. "I'll try to control myself. Where the hell are we going?"

"To my house. I thought that had already been established."

"Do you live in a tree?"

"Yes. I'm a squirrel. Hadn't you noticed?"

Her retort melted on her tongue when the house appeared between the trees. Danny had been so wrong. That was definitely no 'money-eating box of kindle wood.'

Chapter Seven

The white house stood out clearly against the dark forest setting in the fading light, as if he'd planned it that way. It was a wide, two-story house that Duncan had fallen in love with the moment he'd seen it, despite its sad state back then. Warm, welcoming light shone from above the door and there was smoke coming out the chimney. It never failed to make him feel like he was coming *home* and not just returning to a house.

"Wow." Clara turned to look at him as he parked the car. "Do you live above the garage or what?"

He smirked. "Don't give up your day job to become a comedian. You'd starve, baby."

Apparently, out of comebacks, she got out of the car to get a better look at the house. It pleased him immensely that she seemed impressed. When he'd locked the car, he followed and watched her gaze up at the house. Although she'd been on his mind most of the time while he'd transformed it from the less-than-attractive names Danny and Luke had called it and into a real home, he was unprepared for how he felt when he saw her there.

Baby Eve had already been gone by the time Duncan met the Quinns for the first time, but after Bali, they had all unknowingly been searching for the same girl, although in different ways. In some ways, it took Duncan seeing her next to the expensive piece of therapy that had kept him sane to fully realize he'd found her again. Or that she'd found him unknowingly.

"Why does Danny think this place is a dump?" Clara asked, trailing her hand over the porch railing.

"He used to think it was a dump. Everyone did. They were right."

"Did you do it yourself?"

"Pretty much. There was some electrical stuff I needed help with, but other than that, yeah. Come on. Let me show you the inside."

She sent him a teasing smile. "I didn't know you were a handyman. Did you bring me here to show off?"

"Absolutely. And to feed you."

He showed her the house, trying to hide his pride and joy over finally seeing her where he'd imagined her so often. Her obvious awe made him feel like the king of the world, and he tried to see it through her eyes. He'd wanted a home he could live in until the day he died, hopefully of old age. A house where he could raise a family. A house that had ended up being good for his mental health when he'd worked on it, but after almost everything was complete, it just reminded him of the demon he'd been trying to exorcise—the demon now standing in the middle of his living room.

"I can practically see the Christmas stockings hanging on the mantle." Clara smiled as she looked around. "And the floors are amazing, Duncan. Why do you waste your time taking pictures?"

He loved how she made him laugh. "I happen to enjoy my job. I'm good at it."

She nodded as her eyes settled on the large black and white prints he'd hung in black frames on the wall. He'd wanted his family close, so there was a photograph of each of them, all laughing. He'd even managed to snap one of Aunt Tilda on a rare occasion when she was chuckling into a coffee cup.

After the grand tour— she'd been enthralled with the window seat he'd just put in— he told her to sit down at the breakfast bar with a glass of wine while he cooked steaks and roasted some vegetables in the oven.

"Is there anything you can't do? I mean, it's like you're not real."

"Plenty, baby. I can't read your handwriting for instance."

She sighed heavily, making him snicker while he stood with his back turned. "Are you ever going to get over that?" she asked.

"No."

"Well, you're going to have to. It's how I write. It's not my fault that you don't have enough imagination to actually read it."

He grinned as he turned around to face her. "Would it kill you to admit that you wrote it sloppily?"

Humor danced in her eyes, but her mouth remained firm. "It might. Don't insult my handwriting."

"It's not an insult. It's a fact." Duncan kept his gaze locked with hers as he moved toward her. With perfect honesty, he could claim that he hadn't brought her to his house for reasons other than wanting to cook dinner, give her a chance to get out of the hotel room without facing the Quinn inquisition and selfishly, to spend some time with her. But with her sitting at the breakfast bar that he'd put up while trying, unsuccessfully, to exorcise the memory of her from his mind, there was no way he could stay away from her.

The instant his lips were on hers, he knew there was no way he would let her go again. Her taste sent a surge of deep, basic need through him, and he felt a moan bubbling up through his throat. Why the hell hadn't he traveled to Denmark and looked at every one of their young women until he'd found Clara? It was a small country; surely, it wouldn't have been that hard.

He nibbled on her lower lip, breathing in her moans. Then he licked her neck before his lips found her earlobe.

"We can't do this," Clara protested. It sounded a little weak, and the palm on his chest didn't push him away. It was just there. Still, he wasn't an asshole, so he took a step back and started to count to ten in his head. He only got to four.

"Why not?"

"Because..." She downed her wine. "Because we just can't."

"Give me a good reason or I'll kiss you again."

She glared at him. "The hell you will!"

"You're so easy to get riled up." He grinned and grabbed the wine bottle. "Refill? I like the way it tastes on your tongue."

"Duncan, don't do that."

"Do what? I'm just asking if you'd like more wine." He filled her glass and put the bottle back down. He needed both hands to cup her face and make her look at him. "Now, give me that excellent reason for why two single... You *are* single, aren't you?"

She nodded in his hold.

"Good. A reason why two single adults who are attracted to each other can't kiss."

Clara didn't squirm. She didn't look away. "Because we've already messed it up once. I'll be going home soon, then what? Just because you'll have my number this time won't change that we'll be half a world apart. It's easier if we keep a little distance now."

He considered it. "Do you always take the easy way? Because if you do, then you could have let the sheriff handle telling Grace and Carl that you were alive but perfectly content in your new life. You could have written down the number to your local pizza place when I asked for your phone number in Bali."

"Maybe I've wised up since making those decisions."

"Maybe you have. And maybe you're afraid. God knows I'm terrified that you'll disappear into thin air again."

She looked down, struggling against his hands. "I won't disappear, but I will be going home."

"We could work it out."

"How? We both have jobs that depend on us being on opposite sides of the globe." She swallowed. "Duncan, please don't."

"It's a mistake to walk away from this."

"The vegetables are going to burn."

Snorting because of the ridiculousness, Duncan gave her a quick kiss and turned back to his cooking. Clearly, he had to slow down or she'd bolt out the door. "Will you set the table? I'll have the smile back on your face in no time with my culinary skills, then I'll work some more on convincing you that I'm right."

He took it easy on her after that. It was clear she was struggling with whatever was going on in her head, and he'd set out to give her an easy night. Instead of trying his luck again, he told her of his misadventures while working on the house. He had not been much of a handyman initially, but he'd gotten there, been stubborn and worked hard until he figured it out.

They discussed cakes in the living room after dinner. Duncan hadn't been kidding about wanting to impress. Everyone had shaken their heads when he'd bought the house. His birthday would be the first time they all saw it close to complete the way he wanted it. And with Clara there, too. It had to be a success.

"Everybody loves chocolate," Duncan stated. At least he loved chocolate, and it was his damn birthday.

"But wouldn't it be more fun to do something with exotic fruit?" Clara was scrolling on her phone, apparently looking at recipes.

"Why is exotic fruit better than what grows locally? I happen to like apples."

"Boring. At least for a birthday cake."

"Apple pie is boring?"

Again with the raised eyebrows. "You want apple pie?"

"No, I want a cake. A big-ass cake with lots of chocolate."

"Searching for big-ass chocolate cake recipes." She laughed and moved her foot when he reached for it on the couch. He couldn't help trying to touch her all the time. It was an obsession.

"A layer cake?" she suggested. "In Denmark, we always have layer cakes for birthdays. Sponge cake with vanilla cream, raspberry jelly and lots of whipped cream. Sometimes macaroons. Oh, and definitely sprinkles on the icing."

"No chocolate?"

Rolling her eyes, she put the phone away. "I give up. We'll make a chocolate cake with chocolate filling, chocolate frosting and chocolate sprinkles."

"Throw in some chocolate whipped cream and we're golden."

"You are such a child."

"You're allowed to be a child on your birthday." He stretched and was pleased to realize that he'd gotten her to relax and let down her guard. "What's your favorite birthday memory?"

A smile stretched across her tempting lips. "I'm not sure I can choose one. I had a very happy childhood. I suppose being an only child meant that my parents spoiled me a bit. Because we didn't have a big family to invite over for parties, we often had outings on birthdays instead. I was only around ten when I started wanting to go to art museums and galleries. I could spend hours just looking at the paintings. I think my parents were bored out of their skulls to be honest, but they never said anything. Before that, we'd go places like Legoland, the zoo or the aquarium."

"There are few things better than happy childhood memories." Duncan thought about his own childhood, then about Clara's, happy that out of all the alternatives discussed in the Quinn family or whispered about after lights out at night, the one where she was happy with people who loved her had been the real one.

"You have good childhood memories, right? From when you went to live with the Quinns?" she asked, looking at him with a worried expression. He loved her eyes. They showed her soul and everything she was feeling.

"Oh, yeah. Even before…my parents never let me go anywhere, not until Grace went to see them one day and asked if I could come play with her boys. Then it was like they discovered they could just ship me off to the Quinns whenever they wanted. I didn't mind. The Quinn house was like a whole new world. Laughter and cookies and toys and love."

"When I returned to school after the whole thing with the hospital, someone said that they were just trying to replace you with me. It ate at me for days because I didn't want to be anybody's replacement. Finally, Carl lured it out of me. We had a talk unlike any I'd ever had with an adult. He made me feel like his equal. He made me understand that no one could ever replace you, just like no one could ever replace me if they lost me. And you know what? Never once have they made me feel like I wasn't theirs."

"I'm so happy you had them. I wish I knew them like you do. I just can't seem to break that whole Eve barrier, if that makes sense."

He nodded. "I think I know what you mean. Maybe it's because out of everyone, they remember Eve best. So while it's been easier for your siblings to accept that Eve has become Clara, Grace and Carl are just having a harder time with it."

"Yeah, you're probably right. It's difficult when we're coming from completely different angles. They want their Eve and the only one who can give her to them is me. I don't know anything about Eve."

"I know they think they want Eve," he said, reaching for her hand. He was only mildly surprised when she let him take it. "But time doesn't stand still, they've acknowledged that, too, by turning what used to be a nursery into what eventually became a room for a young woman. So they can't get their baby back, but I think you've done your best to show them that at least in some ways, they can have their daughter back."

"I want to give them whatever I can. I want to see them like you do.

It just feels like we're stuck. They want more than they have and I can't give them more than I have."

Duncan had no problem seeing how good things could be between Clara and her birth parents because he knew them so well, but something had to give. Clara had done everything she could. Mama and Papa Q had to stop expecting Eve and to realize what a gem they had in Clara. Her patience wasn't going to last forever. He decided to have a chat with them soon. They'd helped him so much over the years; perhaps it was time he returned the favor.

* * * *

The house felt empty when Duncan returned home after driving Clara back to the hotel. He hated that she was staying at a hotel just as much as the rest of the family did. At first, he'd understood why she didn't just accept the offer to stay in the room that had been hers for all of five months of her life in a house belonging to people she didn't know. He still understood why she didn't want to stay at the Quinn house. Grace and Carl were still struggling to see Clara instead of Eve. But Luke, Danny, and Ben had all offered her their guest bedrooms. Rachel had offered her couch in the small apartment in New Haven she used when she wanted to stay close to campus. And personally, Duncan would have offered her his whole house if he'd thought she'd take it.

He'd enjoyed spending time with her. A big part of him would have loved nothing better than to have continued what they'd started in the kitchen. But just talking to her and being able to look at her was a hell of a lot better than when he thought he'd never see her again. His last conscious thought before he fell asleep was that he wanted more. Much more.

Chapter Eight

Clara had never minded grocery shopping. Not too much anyway. But that was when she'd known the things that were on the shelves. These American grocery stores were full of things she'd never expected even existed. Pie filling in a can? Why didn't they just make their own? Boxes and boxes of powdered mixes for just about everything. Did people actually buy that stuff? Where were the things she actually needed? She was almost relieved when she found the sugar, the flour and the eggs. For a second, she worried that would be canned, too.

Remembering to get plenty of chocolate, she checked her list one more time. Her little shopping expedition had almost taken an hour because she'd been so overwhelmed with the unfamiliar store and the even more unfamiliar items it carried. Curiosity had demanded she look at everything she didn't immediately recognize.

Finally, she had everything she needed to make a chocolate cake for Duncan that would make him go into a chocolate coma. After paying and exiting the store, she was just about to try to find the phone number for a cab company when she realized she didn't know the address of Duncan's house. His birthday was the following day, and he'd promised to cook her dinner again for helping him out with the cake.

Instead of texting him to ask, she walked the short distance to his studio. She'd passed it a few times on her way to Luke's shop, but she'd never been inside. Maybe if she was lucky, she could catch him before he left.

She didn't just catch him, she ran smack into him turning the corner next to the studio.

"Ow." She rubbed her shoulder where it had caught his.

"Damn, baby. I wish you appeared like that, without hurting yourself, every time I thought about you," he said and took the shopping bags from her. "Are you okay?"

"Yeah. If only you weren't built like a brick wall. You've been working out since Bali."

Chuckling, he led her over to his car. "I'm not sure I like the implication that I wasn't in excellent physical form back then."

Clara rolled his eyes. "Males and their egos."

"At least my ego has always been in excellent form."

She laughed. "Can I get a ride? I was just about to call a cab when I realized I don't know the address of your forest hideaway."

"Of course. I was going to swing by the hotel to see if you were there anyway. I didn't know you'd gone shopping so early."

"Honestly? I almost gave up when I saw the inside of the grocery store. Is there anything you can't buy in a can?"

He frowned and held the passenger side door open for her. "What do you mean?"

"I mean that the variety of canned goods is scary."

"I don't think I've ever seen a canned pizza," he offered, starting the car.

"Thank God."

"Pizza dough, however…"

Clara wrinkled her nose. "Ew. Let's change the subject."

He gave her an amused glance as he maneuvered the streets. "You're a food snob."

"Maybe. I'm just not used to food that comes in cans and powdered mixes. My way of cooking is from scratch."

"So no chocolate cake from a box?" he asked.

"Hell no."

It was fun to cook with Duncan, Clara discovered. Although Mrs. Quinn had had a catering business for many years, he hadn't been bragging when he'd said he was almost as good a cook as she was. He could definitely cook more than vegetables and steaks. The most amazing part was how casual he was about it. He'd teased her about the canned nightmare, but he didn't use cans, either. Or even recipes.

"Okay, I think that's as far as I can get today. The rest I'll have to do tomorrow. I'm taking half a day off."

Clara hummed in response and concentrated on the icing swirls she was applying to the cake. He'd wanted a cake, so she was going to make him the most impressive cake she possibly could. A small part of her wanted to impress Mrs. Quinn as well. And the unknown Aunt Tilda. She sounded like a lady who was difficult to impress.

"So, small detail I forgot to consider," Duncan said. He was chopping vegetables that she hoped was for their dinner. She was starving.

"What's that?"

"I'll have to leave that cake alone for twenty-four hours. I'm not sure if I have that kind of willpower."

Clara straightened up and looked at him, unimpressed. "If you touch it before you serve it for your family, I'll... Think of the most painful thing in the world and apply it to you."

He grinned. "God, I love a woman who takes her cakes seriously."

She rolled her eyes. She wasn't convinced he'd leave it alone.

Clara had debated for days what to get Duncan for his birthday. She felt that their history should somehow matter in what she chose for him, but she was unsure of how meaningful to make it. In the end, she'd decided to be honest and give him something that mattered to her and hopefully to him, too.

Borrowing the backroom at Luke's shop, she had picked up a paintbrush for the first time since she'd discovered she might not be who she thought she was. She had painted from her memory, the stunning Bali beach where they'd met and the kids he'd been photographing fishing on the rocks. The colors were a perfect fit for his living room.

On the day of the party, Luke helped her frame it.

"I can't believe how talented you are," he said. "I do a little sketching for fun sometimes, but this..."

She'd always had a difficult time accepting praise, even when a logical part of her could see she deserved it, so she shrugged uncomfortably. "A lot of it is practice."

"And even more of it is talent. Don't sell yourself short."

Smiling wryly, she took a step back to see how the frame looked. "Thank you."

"So is this an actual beach somewhere, or does it only exist in your mind and on this canvas? I want to go there."

"Bali."

"Ohh." Luke whistled. "Well, well, well. Birthday present just got a hell of a lot more meaningful. Beats the boxing gloves I'm getting him."

Clara blew out a breath. "I don't want him to misunderstand. Maybe I'm just being overly sentimental at the moment because it feels like I have no personal history over here. It's like I didn't exist for twenty-seven years. Then at one point during those twenty-seven years, Duncan knew me. I existed."

She ran a hand through her hair, knowing she was rambling but also unable to stop. "Meeting him mattered, and it was hard to accept that he wasn't going to call when he'd said he would. But I got over it. I don't want the painting to say that I didn't."

"One of the good things about Duncan is that he doesn't assume or read into things. If he's uncertain, he asks. So if he doesn't understand the meaning behind your gift, he'll ask you about it." Luke wrapped the painting up expertly while Clara watched.

"Thanks."

He sent her a smile. "You're welcome. Fair warning though—have an honest answer ready if he asks. That painting doesn't scream *friends*. It suggests something more. It still blows my mind that you guys met several years ago and that you're the girl he bitched about giving him a fake phone number. You really got to him."

"It was mutual," she admitted, hoping Duncan would understand the deeper meaning with the picture better than Luke would. "And I'm shutting up now. I just realized that it's an awkward subject to discuss with your brother. It's a first for me, that's why I'm so slow."

Luke laughed. "I've had far worse experiences involving a sister. I've been Rachel's 'Eve stand-in' more times than I can count."

"How so?" She sensed good stories buried there, and she was eager to change the subject.

"Oh, everything from painting my nails to asking me for sex advice. She's the reason Mom and Dad thought I was gay for a while."

"Seriously? That's hilarious."

He winced. "Rachel agrees."

Clara caught a ride with Luke out to Duncan's place. They were the first to arrive, and she had a moment alone with the birthday boy to give him his present when Luke was delegated to drive to the store for napkins.

"Happy birthday," she said and handed Duncan the wrapped painting. "I hope you like it."

"Did you know that I love presents? Like really, really love presents and turn into a little kid when there are presents on the horizon?"

She laughed. "No, I didn't. Sounds like you're a nightmare at Christmas."

"Oh yeah." He ripped the paper off the painting and then spent a really long time just looking at it. Clara got more and more nervous when he didn't say anything.

"Clara… This is… Crappy handwriting forgiven." He looked at her, smiling widely. "For a really long time I thought Bali didn't matter to you at all. But it does. Everything about this picture says it does. Thank you. It's beautiful."

Pleased that she seemed to have gotten her message across, she returned the smile. "You're welcome."

She knew she shouldn't have been surprised when he cupped the back of her head and drew her in for a kiss, not after Luke's warning, but she was. It was a kiss that sent her right back to Bali just like the one in his kitchen a few nights earlier. It was also a kiss she never wanted to end and that never should have begun in the first place.

"Duncan," she murmured through the fire he lit inside of her.

"Clara." Her name was just a breath on his lips before he pulled back, leaving her almost unsteady on her feet and like she'd lost touch with reality for a moment.

Clearing her thoughts, she fought to find something to say. "Do you thank everyone like that?"

He laughed and shook his head. She almost ducked when he reached out to run his fingers through her hair. "No. That kind of thanks is reserved for the most talented, most stubborn and most beautiful women who drive me crazy."

They were too close to the edge. Clara felt like she was going to fall any moment, and she knew it would hurt. "We can't."

"So you keep saying." He nodded, an unreadable expression on his face. "I can be patient when it suits me."

Unwilling to even think about that statement when she knew the house would be crawling with Quinns in a moment, Clara changed the subject and asked to be set to work. Clearly amused, Duncan admitted he'd underestimated the time, so he was happy for her help.

It meant that she was in the kitchen when everyone else arrived, but most of them stuck their head in and said hi. Mrs. Quinn wanted to help, but Duncan didn't allow it. Clara thought it was cute how he wanted to impress her. It was annoying how cute he was. And hot. It would all be so much easier if he'd just turned out to be the asshole she'd expected him to be.

Once everything was ready to be served, Duncan handed her a drink and shooed her out of the kitchen, thanking her for her help.

"I'll make it up to you," he promised her.

She smiled and went toward the murmur of voices.

"Well, let's see her then." Clara heard the unfamiliar voice as she neared the living room and knew it had to be Aunt Tilda since she knew everyone else's voices. She didn't know why, but she was nervous about meeting the old woman. It sounded like she was quite the character.

"Hello." Clara stepped fully into the living room.

"Aunt Tilda, this is our Eve," Mrs. Quinn said, her voice almost breaking.

"Clara," Luke corrected, smiling apologetically at Clara. "Her name is Clara."

"Well, of course. Why would it be Eve when she wasn't raised as Eve Quinn? You never think, Grace. The world is full of people who don't think." Aunt Tilda picked up a pair of glasses that were on a chain around her neck. "Come closer, child. My eyes have seen too much to still be as good as they used to be."

Clara did as asked, feeling as if she were about to take an exam she hadn't studied for. Aunt Tilda was a small, white-haired woman, but her gaze was like a hawk's.

"Well. She does look like Rachel, but are you sure she's not an imposter? The world is full of them."

Swallowing her gasp, Clara didn't have time to object before her own little Quinn army came to her rescue. They were all-insistent and talked at the same time, but Danny was the loudest. "There was a DNA test, Aunt Tilda. Actually, there were two. But Luke would have known without it."

"Luke." Aunt Tilda snorted in the most un-ladylike manner. "That boy dreams. He always has."

"Thanks, Aunty." Luke didn't look bothered with the insult. "But DNA is hard science."

"Unless they made a mistake. Got the samples contaminated. The world is full of useless people."

"Aunt Tilda, we're all sure. Clara is Eve." Mr. Quinn didn't raise his voice, but there was enough authority in it to make Aunt Tilda huff and squint at Clara again.

"Well then. Welcome home, child. Your family all thought you were dead, except that dreamer of a twin brother you have. And me, of course. If there's no body to bury, no one's dead. That's what I always say."

"Thank you, ma'am." Clara made the mistake of looking at Danny, who was rolling his eyes behind Aunt Tilda's back. She had to bite the inside of her cheek not to laugh. "It's very nice to meet you."

"No need for flattery, girl. Carl says you were in Denmark all this time?"

"That's right."

"I never cared much for Denmark. I've seen Copenhagen from the seaside a few times, but I always stayed onboard. They have this free town where they sell drugs on the open street in broad daylight. I've read all about it."

"Christiania. Yes, ma'am. The city has a lot more to offer than that, though."

"Yes, yes. Vikings, beer and that tiny mermaid statue."

Clara smiled. She had no idea if she'd passed the exam, but she liked the old woman despite how freely she spoke her mind. "Among other things, yes. If you ever find yourself entering Danish waters again, give me a call. I'll show you a Copenhagen you didn't know existed."

Aunt Tilda narrowed her eyes. "No bars."

"No bars."

Seemingly pleased, the old woman nodded. "Duncan? Are we ever going to eat? A woman could starve around here without anyone noticing. The world is full of starving people, so why add to that number?"

"Dinner is ready, Aunt Tilda," Duncan replied. "May I escort you to the table?"

"Why?" She looked up at him suspiciously. "You think I can't find my own way? Your house is big, but not that big. Nowhere near as big as a cruise ship."

"I was only trying to be helpful." Clara could see that Duncan was trying not to laugh.

"When men are helpful, they want something. You already got your birthday present, so move out of my way. I'm starving. I hope you didn't order pizza or something. The world is full of people who can't cook, but they better not be Quinns. Or Cantwells."

Duncan pulled out the chair for her even though it made her scowl. "I'm too afraid of you to serve pizza, Aunt Tilda. God's honest truth."

"Good."

"Is she always like that?" Clara whispered to Luke.

"Pretty much. Except when she's in a bad mood. Then she's worse. She grows on you, though... Like fungus."

She giggled. "You're so bad."

"Nah. Just honest."

Like every other meal Clara had shared with the Quinns, Duncan's birthday dinner was loud, funny and slightly confusing. Everyone talked at the same time. Half the time she had no idea what they were discussing.

Aunt Tilda kept a running commentary on what the world was full of. Even though she seemed to be reluctant to offer too much praise, because the world was full of people with large egos, she had seconds of everything and told Duncan that he was allowed to cook for her again sometime. Duncan beamed as if he'd been awarded a Michelin star.

It was very interesting to watch him, Clara discovered. There was so much more to him than met the eye. Part of him thrived on living alone in the forest and another part of him belonged in the center of a large family, who showered him with attention, love and gifts on his birthday. It was hard to imagine him as a little boy, unwanted and unloved. She didn't know if Mr. and Mrs. Quinn had been more receptive to sensing another child hurting because they were afraid for her, but she was glad they'd gotten Duncan away from his parents.

"The world is full of loud people," Aunt Tilda said, startling Clara out of her thoughts.

Clara smiled and agreed. Apparently, Aunt Tilda was deaf to her own voice when she wanted to be heard, which she did often. "Where were you on your last cruise, Miss Quinn? It sounds exciting to be traveling so much."

"I appreciate the lifestyle," Aunt Tilda replied, seemingly pleased to be talking about herself. Clara thought she was adorable. "I went to the Mediterranean. I don't like the cold anymore. When you get to be my age, you only go the places you want to go. Besides, I like Greece."

Unaware that she'd started an avalanche, Clara listened to Aunt Tilda tell her why she liked Greece so much, until the meal was over. More than once, the Greek men's physique was mentioned.

After dinner, Clara chose to play with Tommy and Leanne for a bit. She had a headache, and trying to keep up with conversation when everybody talked at the same time about things she didn't know anything about, didn't help. It wasn't just topics relating to a past she hadn't been part of that made her feel excluded. She also knew very little about American politics and popular culture. As she'd already discovered, the media's way of portraying America wasn't always as close to the truth as she'd experienced personally.

The kids were getting sleepy though. Leanne quickly fell asleep on a throw pillow behind the couch. Tommy crawled into Clara's lap and sleepily told her a story about a blue racecar and a donkey without ears. He was adorable, and there was certainly nothing wrong with his imagination. When he'd dozed off, too, she helped Ben tuck the kids into Duncan's bed until it was time for them to go home.

She forced herself not to take in too many details of the bedroom. In her weary state of mind, she was slightly afraid of where her thoughts might go.

The cake was a success. Aunt Tilda wanted to know where Duncan had bought it, and Danny looked like someone had kicked his puppy when Luke took the last piece.

"Can you bake a cake for my birthday, too?" Rachel begged. Clara couldn't even answer because if she'd ever been told when her younger sister's birthday was, she'd forgotten it. Soon, she'd be back home without any idea when she'd be visiting next.

Luke drove her back to her hotel after a long night. She was asleep on her feet. He laughed at her when she almost walked into the glass door.

"Be careful. No one looks attractive with a broken and bloody nose."

"Oh, I don't know. There are some pretty hot boxers out there who could probably pull it off." She giggled sleepily; feeling almost drunk although she'd only had a glass of wine before her headache made her switch to water.

"Yes, but you're not a boxer, are you?" Luke patiently steered her from the elevator to her room.

"No, I'm more a kicking shins and pulling hair kind of girl," she admitted and shook herself out of it so she could unlock the door. "Thanks for the ride, Luke."

"Anytime." He smiled nervously and handed her a leather-bound journal-looking book. "I was wondering... Would you take a look at this sometime?"

"Sure," she agreed easily and turned it over in her hands. "What is it?"

"It's the stuff I was telling you about a while ago. Everyone thinks I'm crazy, but when I felt something that didn't feel...natural, you might say, I wrote it down. You have the final verdict, sis. Tell me if I'm crazy or if I had a connection to you somehow."

Clara suddenly felt fully awake. She hadn't forgotten he'd mentioned the journal before, and she wasn't blind to what he trusted her with. Looking down at the journal, she took a deep breath before looking back up at him. "I'll read it. But Luke? The way you came rushing in that first day... No matter what's in this journal, I believe in the connection. Even though I haven't felt it the same way you have, I'd rather be called crazy with you than have missed out on that experience. You freaked me out a bit, but you had different expectations of me than everyone else. You instantly understood that I wasn't Eve—*couldn't* be Eve. That meant everything to me."

He nodded. "Let me know, though, okay?"

"Of course."

Clara had expected sleep to come instantly when she was buried under the covers a short time later. But it didn't. She had a book to read.

Chapter Nine

While doing the last bit of cleaning after the previous night's party, Duncan decided the house must have expanded while he'd been asleep. It certainly felt that way when it was just him around compared to the whole family the night before. He considered getting a dog just for the company. He didn't even like dogs.

When the house was as clean as it was going to get, he removed the artwork above the fireplace and replaced it with Clara's painting. Then he dumped himself on the couch with a cup of coffee and looked at it.

She'd captured everything he remembered about it. He had photos of it, of course, but even on his best days, he couldn't get as much life and soul into a simple beach scene. Clara could. He almost expected to be able to hear the waves, to smell the saltwater and the sunscreen. Smell her. Feel her.

Sighing, he realized that maybe having the painting where he could see it every day wasn't such a good idea. It was stunning, but the memories might prove to be a bit too much to deal with. Then he snorted. The memories were there anyway, painting or no painting. He wasn't going to be satisfied with memories anyway. He wanted the real thing.

With no plans and not being the type to laze around on the couch all day, he didn't mind when his phone rang. It was Mama Q, who asked him to stop by to look at a leaky pipe. Since starting to fix up his house, Duncan had become the go-to guy for all things practical. He didn't mind. It gave him something to rub in his brothers' faces. Besides, he'd no doubt score lunch. Not a bad paycheck.

* * * *

Aunt Tilda was telling Mama Q how to bake muffins when he entered the Quinn home. His favorite and only aunt had her own house, but she never used it. When she wasn't sailing around the world, she stayed with her nephew and his wife.

"Good morning, ladies," he greeted them.

"It's not morning, you rascal. We don't all snooze till noon." Aunt Tilda only spared him a fleeting glance. "Not so much sugar, Grace!"

"Hello, dear." Mama Q put down the bag of sugar and gave Duncan a hug. "Thanks for coming over so quick. Carl is out playing golf or I would have had him look at it. I'm afraid it might get worse and flood the basement."

"I'm on it."

It turned out to be a quick fix, and as long as he kept an eye on it in the future, he didn't think it would be an issue. He went back up to the kitchen, where he distracted Aunt Tilda with questions about her latest trip so Mama Q could make her muffins in peace.

"What's wrong with you?" Aunt Tilda asked when Duncan had run out of questions.

"What do you mean? I'm fine."

She huffed. "Obviously not, young man. Why aren't you married yet?"

He couldn't stop the laughter. "With all due respect to women and their age, you're older than me, Aunt Tilda. At least by a year or two. Why aren't you married?"

"That's different." She pressed her lips together.

"How so?"

"Because I never wanted to get married. You do."

"I do?" he asked, wondering who had stamped that on his forehead without him noticing.

"Yes. A man doesn't make himself a house like you've done without wanting a family. For that you need a wife."

"Unless I adopt a couple of orphans and get thirty cats."

She stared at him. "You're crazy enough to do that, I'll give you that much. You're also avoiding the subject, so I know I'm right. I usually am. The world is full of people who think they're right without actually being it, but I'm not one of them."

"Stop pestering the boy. I made lunch." Mama Q came to Duncan's rescue. He stood up to help with the plates.

"It was a lovely party last night, Duncan. I love that at least one of my kids listened when I tried to teach you guys to cook," she said when they were seated and Aunt Tilda was busy inspecting her lunch.

"Thanks. Getting a real kitchen has helped. The one at the loft was difficult to work with."

"More like impossible, dear. You didn't even have a proper oven."

He grinned. "I got by. But I do enjoy cooking now."

"Personally, I liked the cake the best." Aunt Tilda pushed the salad away from the rest of her food. "Plenty of people in the world who can cook. Not a lot who can bake anything worth eating."

"I regret not saving a piece for today," Duncan said, grinning. The chocolate dream of a cake had been the single most amazing thing he'd ever eaten.

"Do you think she might want to part with the recipe?" Mama Q asked. "It really was spectacular."

"Wouldn't hurt to ask." He might have to ask for it himself. He'd never had much luck baking, but for that cake, he'd give it another go. Trying to charm her into giving him a tutorial could be fun, too.

"I'm going to take a nap just this once," Aunt Tilda declared after lunch. Her idea of 'just this once' was every day.

"Want me to tuck you in?" Duncan grinned and was pleased to see Aunt Tilda's lips form a quick smile before she scowled at him.

"Rascal."

"I'll take that as a no. Sweet dreams, Aunty."

No sooner had Aunt Tilda closed the door to the guest bedroom upstairs, then Papa Q appeared in the kitchen. "I heard her say she was going to take a nap, so I waited a minute before coming in," he said as they laughed at him.

"Scared of an old woman. You're such an amazing role model," Duncan told him.

"You avoid her, too." Carl kissed his wife and grabbed a cup of coffee before sitting down at the table.

"You two are terrible," Grace scolded them.

"Who made sure you could bake your muffins in peace?" Duncan reminded her.

"Oh, God. You're right." She laughed. "Thanks, dear."

Duncan sipped his coffee and stretched out his legs under the table. "I actually wanted to talk to you about something."

"Is something wrong?" Mama Q looked at him like she'd done since he was a kid, checking him for possible injuries. Like a real mom. It warmed him from the top of his head to the soles of his feet.

"No," he assured her quickly. "Nothing's wrong. I was just wondering how you were handling everything with Clara."

"Oh." They looked at each other before Papa Q cleared his throat. "Getting our daughter back is a miracle. To be praying for something that long, then have her walk through the door... There's no other way to describe it. Of course, all that time gave us—*all* of us—time to imagine all kinds of things. Most of them bad, because that's what experts told us to expect, but also many happy ones. Yet reality is nothing like anything we'd ever imagined."

They looked at each other again, Mama Q with a frown on her face. "It's not a disappointment, please don't think that. It's just difficult to accept that she's not ours anymore. I mean, all our kids are adults now, but they're still ours. Eve, however... We only had her for five months and even though she's back, she's not ours."

Duncan nodded thoughtfully. "I see what you mean. I can also see things from Clara's perspective. Part of her is miserable. She's given all she can, and she still feels like you want more."

"All I've ever done is fail her." Mama Q pressed her fist against her lips.

"That's not true." Duncan and Papa Q said it at the same time.

"Yes, it is. I let someone take her when she was a baby. Now I can't even see that she's hurting."

"Grace. I thought you were past the guilt."

Duncan felt like he was intruding on a private moment. He felt bad about making Mama Q cry.

"I'm sorry. I didn't mean to make you feel bad. I just hate seeing the three of you struggle. You need Clara as much as she needs you."

"You care." She brushed the tears away. "About Eve."

"First of all, if you ever expect to get closer to her, you need to start calling her *Clara*. I know she was your Eve for five months, but she's been Clara for twenty-seven years. Secondly, yes, I do care about her."

"Calling her Clara is just another reminder that she isn't ours." Mama Q sighed. "There's just so much distance, almost as if there's still a world between us. Years ago, Stacy next door complained that her kids called her by her first name. My daughter calls me Mrs. Quinn."

"Maybe Mrs. Quinn and Eve have to go away," Duncan suggested gently. "I have a feeling that Grace and Clara could start out by becoming friends. I know there's no way I can imagine what any of you are feeling, but I'd just like to remind you that it's probably easier for Clara, who has grown up as an only child, to accept siblings than it is for her to replace the parents she lost. I know it isn't fair, but it's human emotions. It makes sense if you think about it."

"It does," Papa Q replied. He was clutching Mama Q's hand.

"The worst part should be over. We have her back, but in some ways, it's as bad as it was before when we didn't know where she was. It just hurts." She wiped away more tears. "Every reminder that someone else had her is like a stab in the heart. Every little thing I don't know about her is just as bad. No matter what I do, I'll never catch up."

"No. None of us will ever catch up, but to a certain degree, we could try. Did any of you watch Clara last night? Really watch her?"

Duncan watched them both shake their heads. "Do you remember some of the things we all talked about?"

"Some of your past birthdays," Mama Q replied. "The election."

"We also talked about that holiday we took to Florida the first summer you were with us," Papa Q added.

"Clara ended up playing with the kids because she can't catch up either," Duncan said. "She's struggling every bit as much as you are, except she's alone and you have each other. I know you and love you—and I know Clara. You'd be better off struggling together than struggling alone."

They both nodded, and Mama Q reached over to squeeze his hand. "We will try. Thank you, dear."

He smiled and hoped they'd figure it out. More than anything, he wished he could just fix it for them, but he'd done all he could.

"Duncan? You really do care a lot about her, don't you?"

Mama Q was the only true mother he'd ever had. The one who had given him life didn't count. Life did not mean love. Mama Q had that mother gene, the one that enabled her to see things he was trying to hide. The one that made it next to impossible to lie to her, and if he did, she'd certainly see right through him.

"Yes, I really do," he admitted. "I have for a long time. I'm sorry I haven't told you before, but I knew her as Clara before I had any idea she used to be a baby called Eve."

"What?"

"How?"

"Remember when I was on that assignment in Bali?"

"The one that somehow changed you irrevocably? Made you brood for months, buy a house no one could see the possibilities in but you and grow into a man? Yes, I should think so," Mama Q replied and hesitated a few seconds. "That was because of Clara?"

He wasn't aware he'd been so obvious, but he couldn't deny it, so he nodded. "It messed me up. I thought we had something special, but then I came home and discovered she'd given me a fake phone number. I'd finally accepted that I'd never see her again when she turned up as your Eve. The phone number wasn't fake. I'd just read a digit wrong."

"You and Ev—Clara?" Mama Q looked almost shocked. Papa Q was mirroring her expression.

Duncan couldn't blame them. It had been so easy to be Clara and Duncan, but being Clara, formerly Eve, and Duncan was messy. He considered Luke, Danny and Ben his brothers and Rachel his sister. Grace and Carl were his parents. Clara was the biological sister and child to the Quinns.

"But you never said anything…"

"No." He thought back to the moment he'd walked into the living room and seen her. He'd received Luke's text and been excited to finally meet the elusive Eve then the conflicting emotions when he'd recognized Clara. Elation had come first, then anger, disbelief and suspicion that it was all an elaborate plot to mess with his head even more. Realization and then finally acceptance, acceptance that he had wasted a lot of time and money on the house he had used as therapy. He wasn't over her. Not by a long shot.

"At first, before we had a chance to clear the air, we weren't very happy with each other. I thought she'd given me a fake phone number and she thought I'd been ignoring her. We'd been forced to accept that we'd never see each other again. So much else was going on and had priority."

"And now?" Mama Q asked.

"Now…" Duncan hesitated. He had no idea if they would think it weird or wrong if he admitted that he wasn't letting her go without an epic fight this time. Maybe it was best to wait to tell them until he had gauged their views on it better. "Two years is a long time. I'm just enjoying spending time with her again. So there's nothing to tell."

"Duncan, we both know you better than that." Mama Q had on her no nonsense face. Papa Q was trying not to smile, knowing that if she noticed, he'd get the no nonsense face, too.

"I'm serious. There's nothing to tell. I do wonder what could have been, but Clara has enough to deal with at the moment, so I'm backing off." It was partly a lie, but he couldn't exactly tell them about the scorching kiss in his kitchen earlier that week.

"It's quite a surprise, son." Papa Q reached for his coffee cup. "It's a damn shame that you couldn't decipher her phone number. We could have had her back sooner."

"If you're trying to pin it on Clara or me that you feel like you wasted two years, the—"

"I'm not! Good grief, Duncan." Papa Q rubbed his forehead. "Like Grace said before, reminders that Eve isn't ours hurt. Other people raised her, loved her. Luke had that connection with her all along, Danny was in the same country as her and you actually knew her before she came here. I'm not jealous or bitter. I'm just desperate for some kind of in, an opening if you will. A way to connect with my little girl."

"Talk to her," Duncan urged, hating that he'd upset them. "She's your daughter. Strong, warm and creative like her mother. Emphatic, smart and loving like her father. You may not know the details of her life, but you know her heart."

Duncan was a little shaken when he left the Quinn house later. He hoped he'd gotten his message through, but he hadn't expected things to get so emotional. Aunt Tilda coming back down after her nap had put a stop to the personal conversation. He'd felt too drained to deal with any more lectures of what the world was full of.

He wasn't in the mood to go home, so he drove over to Luke's place after picking up some beer. He'd have closed up his store by now and there was probably a game on TV.

There was. Duncan walked right in like he usually did and found Clara yelling something in what he assumed was Danish at the TV screen, while Luke was trying to stuff a whole slice of pizza into his mouth.

"Are you kidding me? They can do that?" Clara asked, looking wide-eyed at her brother.

"It's a contact sport," Luke managed to reply through the pizza.

"So is soccer. You know, *real* football. But they don't trample each other and get away with it."

Luke shrugged. "Civilized is boring."

"You would say that, considering how you eat. Pig."

Luke grinned and then noticed Duncan, who was trying to hold in his laughter at the easy banter between the reunited twins. No one would guess they hadn't grown up together.

"Hey, Dunc! Just in time with the beer. Sit down and share the goods."

"You just want the beer, dude. Hey, Clara. Enjoying football?"

She snorted. "Hi. It's not football. It's not even a ball. It's an egg."

Duncan sat down and clutched his chest. "No insulting the sport. That's just mean."

"I've been trying to explain the rules," Luke said and opened a beer.

"But he's not very good at explaining things," Clara added.

"Yes, I am!"

Her eyes sparkled and Duncan chuckled, watching the twins instead of the game.

"Explain the offside rule in soccer then," Clara demanded.

Duncan's chuckles became a full-blown grin. Luke didn't know the rules of soccer, although Danny had been trying to teach him pretty much his whole life. He also didn't know when to back down, so he started a complicated and completely wrong explanation that had Clara and Duncan howling with laughter.

Chapter Ten

Clara felt like time was running out. She had a flight to Copenhagen five days later, was scheduled to return to work after two days at home battling jetlag and she still hadn't told anyone. Luke had asked her how long she'd be staying and she'd honestly replied that she didn't know. That was then, when she hadn't known she'd be using up her four full weeks, which was what the high school had given her when she'd asked for time off.

Part of her dreaded leaving her new family. The easy but amazingly strong bond with Luke, flirting with Duncan, settling into siblinghood with Danny, Ben and Rachel. Testing the boundaries with Mr. and Mrs. Quinn.

Another part couldn't wait to sleep in her own bed, not feel guilty every time she wanted an hour to herself and to slip back into the rhythm of big city life. She had left her life behind, and there was unsettled business with the friends who hadn't agreed with her decision to stir up the past. She'd been angry with them because it had been her decision. They had been disappointed with her. She needed to figure out if there was something to salvage from those friendships.

She sighed and looked out the hotel window. She hadn't expected that she might want to stay longer. For some reason, it had never crossed her mind.

Her cell phone beeped with a message. It was Rachel telling her she was waiting downstairs. They were spending Rachel's class-free day together in New London. Clara sometimes had a difficult time dividing her time between everyone who wanted to spend time with her. She wanted to get to know everyone, but when she was tired, confused and on information overload, it was easiest just to call Luke or Duncan. They were the only two she could fully relax around and even with Duncan; it was difficult because of their chemistry. It was clear he wanted more and if Clara was honest, so did she. Fear won out over desire, though. She'd fought hard to get over him once and that was enough.

Rachel's good mood was contagious. She chattered on about anything and everything. If she noticed that Clara was quieter than normal, she didn't comment on it.

"Did Luke ever tell you about when he ran away from home because he wanted to find you?" Rachel asked. She'd barely taken a breath after telling Clara about the assignment she'd just handed in the previous day.

The corner of Clara's mouth lifted into a half smile. Luke and his never-faltering belief. Reading his journal had left her rattled. She still hadn't talked to him about it. "No. Did he make your parents worry?"

"Oh yeah. I don't remember it because I was just a baby, but Danny loves telling the story," Rachel replied. "Luke was around seven or eight. He'd gotten into his head that whoever took you had taken the wrong baby. You were in the same carriage that day, you know. So Luke packed a little bag and took off. His plan was to trade himself for you once he found your kidnapper. He was missing for fourteen hours before someone spotted him sleeping under a bench and called the police. Mom and Dad were freaking out."

"No wonder! Something awful could have happened to him. It's sweet, though." Clara sighed. "Wasn't it hard growing up with a shadow sister?"

"In some ways, yes. I was never allowed to go anywhere alone. Even now, the boys are reluctant to let me do my own thing. It was frustrating, but I understood. Shadow is a good word for it. I usually call it 'The Shadow of Eve.' It's ingrained into the family. Even at our happiest, there was always that little 'if only Eve could have been here, it would have been perfect' thought in our heads."

"I'm really grateful to Mom and Dad that they never made you a taboo. That would have been devastating. You see so many people trying to deal with grief by acting like it's not there, but inside it grows like a cancer. We've always talked about you naturally and openly. It helped to keep the hope alive, too. It's the main reason I'd like to work as a grief counselor. Not everyone is able to handle it the way Mom and Dad did and not try to bury it, but actually talk about it."

Clara had never heard a bad word said about her biological parents. It frustrated her that she couldn't seem to connect with them. "Sounds like an interesting path to take," she told Rachel. "With your own experience, I'm sure it would be a great match for you."

"I'm hoping." She smiled. "I just have to convince everyone that I'm serious about it. I've changed my mind a few times about which career path to follow."

"That probably just means you've thought about it carefully. No harm in that."

"God, Clara. Even without practice, you're still the perfect big sister. Do you have any idea how much grief the rest of the family has given me because I couldn't decide before?"

Clara laughed. "Call it personal experience. For a long time, it didn't even occur to me that I could make art my career. I loved it more than anything, but my brain kept telling me I needed something more solid and reliable. I considered becoming a nurse or a pharmacist for a long time before my mom asked why I didn't just become an art teacher. I'd never felt so dumb before for not thinking of that myself."

"You'd probably heard too much about starving artists."

"Probably."

"Okay, we're here." Rachel parked in a semi-full parking lot. "Let's go shopping. We need to work up an appetite for lunch. I know the most darling little place where they have the best clam chowder. Come on."

Shopping with Rachel was fun. She hadn't spent a lot of time with Rachel alone before, but she discovered they were a lot alike. Except that even on the biggest sugar rush, she'd never become as peppy as Rachel. It wasn't annoying. Rachel was a mood booster.

"I don't know how I lived for so long without knowing what clam chowder was," Clara said when they walked out of the restaurant after lunch. "It sucks when you realize you've been missing out."

Rachel laughed. "Told ya."

Clara sighed and stopped to retrieve her cell phone from her purse when she heard it beep. It was a message from Luke. She started reading but never got to the end before squealing tires, a sickening thump and a car horn honking insistently made her look up.

"Rachel!" Her sister was on the ground, eyes closed and with blood gushing from her forehead. The driver of the car a few yards away from her sat frozen behind the wheel, and for a second Clara didn't think she would be able to move either.

Except she had to.

She ran over to Rachel and kneeled next to her, calling her name. There was no reaction and holding her breath, she checked her sister's pulse. When she felt it strong and steady under her fingertips, she released the breath she'd been holding. The noiseless vacuum she hadn't even realized she'd been in faded away.

"Is she okay?"

"I'm calling an ambulance."

"The car was driving way too fast."

"Shit, that's a lot of blood."

Clara turned her head as her brain was assaulted by faceless voices. A crowd was gathering around them and a man kneeled down next to her, holding a cell phone.

"I've called 911," he told her. "Does she have a pulse?"

Clara nodded, ashamed that someone else had thought of it before she had.

The man spoke into his phone, but she couldn't focus on what he was saying. She took off her scarf and gently pressed it against the gushing wound on Rachel's forehead, carefully avoiding moving her head.

Oh God, why didn't she wake up?

It seemed like forever before the ambulance came, although Clara couldn't clearly remember the time passing. Fear was choking her, and she was certain she would never be able to erase from memory the sight of her unconscious, bleeding sister lying on the road.

The police also showed up, but Clara had nothing to tell them since she'd been looking down at her phone when the car hit Rachel. The man who had called 911 had seen the whole thing, as did a few others. The driver of the car had not moved from his seat, and a police officer was talking to him. Clara had no sympathy for the driver even though he looked like he was frozen in shock. She'd overheard the witnesses telling the police that he'd been driving way too fast on the narrow side street.

Clara rode in the ambulance with Rachel to the hospital. It wasn't until she'd been told to wait in a waiting room that she realized she had some very unpleasant phone calls to make. She was bad luck. First, she caused her family grief for twenty-seven years, and then she had to tell them their sister and daughter had been in an accident.

She wanted to just call Luke and let him deal with the rest, but she knew the first phone call had to be to Mr. and Mrs. Quinn. She was going to make her biological mother cry. Again.

"Quinn Residence."

The sound of Mrs. Quinn's voice made tears form in Clara's eyes. *Mom.* The word wanted to escape from her lips, but she couldn't very well skip straight from Mrs. Quinn to Mom.

"It's Clara." She cleared her throat when it constricted painfully.

"Hello, dear." The smile made it through the phone. Clara could see it clearly in her mind. "Are you and Rachel having fun shopping?"

"No." She struggled to get her voice under control as she heard Mrs. Quinn's gasp. "There was an accident... Rachel was hit by a car. They're treating her now, but she was unconscious and... Oh God. She was bleeding from a head wound."

The broken sob broke Clara's heart. "Oh, dear God, no. I'll get Carl. We're on our way. You're at the hospital in New London?"

"Yes."

Next, she called Luke, who also said he was on his way with Duncan. Because he could read her like no one else, he said he'd call Danny and Ben. That left her alone with her worry and muddled thoughts. And bloody hands. As soon as she noticed, she hurried to the bathroom to wash them. She shuddered as the reddish water swirled down the drain. Rachel had to be okay. She just had to.

Afterward, she found a chair in the corner of the waiting room and sat down. There were a lot of people around, but it was easy to ignore them. She kept her eyes trained on the door, hoping that a doctor would materialize quickly or that her family would show up.

Her family.

Clara closed her eyes and let the overwhelming feelings wash over her for a moment. They truly were her family. Her sister, her brothers... When she opened her eyes again, she knew there was no way she could leave right then. Not when Rachel was hurt, and not when it didn't feel like the right time to leave.

She trembled inside, but her hands were steady when she found her phone and dialed the high school she worked at back home. Getting patched through to her boss, who luckily hadn't left for the day yet, she asked for an extended leave. When she was denied, she asked him to fire her. If she quit, she still had three months leave. Being fired meant she didn't have to go back.

"Are you sure, Clara?" he asked her quietly.

He was a great principal, and Clara had always respected him. But she didn't hesitate when she told him she was sure. She would miss the kids she taught, but for the first time in years, she had to put her own needs first. She hadn't even taken more than a week off when her parents died. The time had come for family.

She'd just canceled her flight on the airline's website when Luke came running in, closely followed by Duncan. Relief surged through her, both because the decision had been made and because of the familiar faces.

"How is she? Have you seen her?" Luke wrapped Clara up in a hug. "Were you hurt?"

Allowing herself a couple of seconds of comfort, she took a deep breath. Because of the height difference between them, she could only just peek over Luke's shoulder at Duncan. He looked like he needed a hug, too.

"I don't know. I'm still waiting for a doctor. And no. Rachel was ahead of me. I didn't even see it because I was trying to read your text. I just heard it," she replied, pulling away from Luke.

Reliving the sound of Rachel's accident in her head made her sick to her stomach. She quietly walked into Duncan's arms and allowed herself another moment of comfort.

They sat down, but Luke couldn't stay still. "I'm going to find a doctor," he announced and jumped back up.

"You okay?" Duncan asked when they were alone.

"I wasn't hurt."

He took her hand, enveloping it completely in his own. "That's not what I meant."

Despite her worry, her lips curved slightly. She couldn't possibly put into words everything she was feeling—sick to her stomach worrying about Rachel, the sound of the car hitting her sister stuck in a loop in her head and the fact that she'd just quit her job to stay in America longer. Not to mention how it made her feel to have her hand encased in his warm, strong grip. On the other hand, she wanted to be honest.

Faced with an impossible task, she simply shrugged. "I just wish someone would come out and tell us that she's okay."

"Yeah," he agreed, rubbing circles on the back of her hand with his thumb. "I also wish you'd answer my question."

She looked at him. "I'm sorry. I *am* okay. Just…worried and overwhelmed. I keep hearing the car hitting her in my head. It's horrible."

"She'll be okay. Rachel is hard-headed. Ben and Danny once dropped her on her head from the apple tree in the yard. She didn't even cry."

He said it so matter-of-factly that it made her gasp. "They did what?"

A chuckle escaped him. "They were playing circus, I think. Rachel was the acrobat. They ended up dropping her while she was hanging with her head down. Rachel got a concussion. Ben and Danny lost their TV privileges for a couple of weeks."

"Maybe I should be grateful that I grew up an only child."

"Might have saved you a cracked skull."

Luke came back with a doctor at the same time as Mr. and Mrs. Quinn arrived. Clara stayed in the background even though she eagerly hung onto every word the doctor said.

"Rachel has a concussion and a deep gash on her forehead that required fourteen stitches. That's why we'll be keeping her overnight for observation. She also has a broken wrist and bruising on her entire left side," he told them. "However, she's awake and is already begging to be released. I told her it's in her best interest to stay overnight so we can be completely satisfied there's nothing to worry about concerning her concussion."

"Stubborn mule," Luke muttered, but the relief shone through his words.

Suddenly beyond exhausted, Clara plopped down into the chair again when the doctor left. She'd never known relief like that before, which just proved how much she had come to care about her new family. Mr. and Mrs. Quinn—she really had to stop calling them that—went to see Rachel, and Luke and Duncan were on the phone sharing the good news with Ben and Danny.

Clara was half asleep an hour later, seated in the passenger seat of Luke's car on the way back to Stonebridge. They'd dropped Duncan off at Rachel's car so he could drive it back.

"What a day." Clara was too tired to process it all. The last bit of energy left her body when she'd seen with her own eyes that Rachel was awake and her biggest worry was if she would end up with a scar.

"Never a dull moment. Are you okay? You look kind of bombed."

"Thanks. You know how to make a girl feel pretty."

He chuckled. "Sorry. But it's true."

"Then I look how I feel." Clara sighed and opened her eyes. "Hey, when you offered me your guest bedroom, you said I could take you up on it anytime. That still true?"

"Of course. Did you finally get enough of the hotel?"

"Yeah." She didn't mention that without a steady income and having to rely on selling her art, she would have to be smart about her finances. Staying at a hotel wasn't smart when you had a twin brother who had offered his guest bedroom at least twenty times. Maybe she could help out at his shop so she wouldn't be a complete freeloader.

"Awesome. We'll pick up your stuff right away."

"Thanks." She smiled tiredly at him.

"It's about time," he replied.

She nodded, not knowing if he saw. It was not the only thing that was about time. It was also about time that she talked to him about the journal. The only reason she hadn't yet was that she was trying to piece together a time line that fit what he'd written down. There was no doubt the connection was very real, but she wanted him to have proof—more than just her words. She wanted to write it down for him, too. Plus, she'd been trying to remember if she had ever had any experiences like the ones he'd recorded. Unexplained feelings that might have been a connection to Luke. It would only be reasonable to assume that the connection went both ways.

Chapter Eleven

"What do you mean *canceled*?" Duncan knew it wasn't Emily's fault, but he had a lot riding on the photo shoot. The last thing he needed was the model not showing up as planned.

"The agency didn't give any details except that she's sick. They also have no one to replace her today."

"But I need it done today. The deadline…" He blew out a breath and forced himself to stop yelling. Emily was just delivering a message.

"I can try another agency, but there aren't a lot of local options," she offered weakly.

"What about Rachel?" Peter interrupted. "You used her for that magazine photo shoot last year when the model showed up drunk."

Duncan turned around. "We really have all the luck when it comes to models, don't we? But it won't work this time. Rachel was in an accident last week and is sporting a bandage on her forehead and a cast on her arm."

"Damn," Peter muttered. "What about Emily?"

"No way," Emily protested. "Not one single picture has been taken of me in the last five years. That's not changing today."

Duncan smiled when it hit him. "I've got it. Clara. I just need to talk her into it."

"Does she have any modeling experience?" Emily asked. "And what about a work permit?"

"A little," he replied, thinking about the pictures she'd let him take of her in Bali. "As for a work permit, it's just photos for what's-his-name, the designer's portfolio or whatever he's calling it. We'll say she did it for free. Most new designers don't hire models and photographers anyway. What's-his-name said so."

Emily nodded. "Sounds like a plan. And his name is Lawrence."

Duncan went into his office for privacy before he dialed Clara's number. Her real number. It was such a nice thing to be able to do. He enjoyed it every time.

"Hello?"

"Hey, it's Duncan. You busy this afternoon?"

"Well, I was planning to work on world peace, but I suppose that can be postponed until tomorrow."

"I'm honored to rate above impossible tasks."

She laughed.

He loved that sound—he wanted to hear it all the time. "I need a favor."

"Okay. What's the favor?"

"I have a photo shoot this afternoon. Deadline's tomorrow and the model canceled."

"Yes…?" The hesitation in her voice was clear.

"I just need you to put on some clothes made by a local designer and let me snap some pictures. It will take a couple of hours, tops."

"You want me to model? Are you insane?"

"My sanity's fine, thank you. And why not? You're beautiful, I already know the camera loves you and I really, really need your help."

"But I can't, Duncan. I'm not a model."

"I'm not looking for someone to walk down a catwalk. I just need you to smile. I know you can smile. I know it looks beautiful when you do. Please?"

"Flatter will get you absolutely nowhere," she said and then sighed.

"Rachel did it last year," he tried to coax her. "She's not a model any more than you are, but the result was amazing."

"Then ask her!"

"I need someone without a bandaged forehead."

"Oh. Right. You'll owe me for the rest of your life, you know that, right?"

He grinned because he knew he had her. "Oh, I don't mind being your humble servant for life."

"You're a lot of things, Duncan, but you're not humble. I'm on my way. Fair warning, I may decide on the walk to your studio that I hate you."

"Thanks for the warning."

He smiled when he ended the call. It had been a lot of fun making Clara pose for pictures in Bali. They were still some of his favorite pictures. He hoped he could bring out the part of her that the camera had loved so much again.

An hour later, he realized he'd been too optimistic. He was also pretty sure that Clara did, in fact, hate him.

"Come on, Clara. Smile, please."

"I am."

"Ah, no, baby. That's not a smile. That's a grimace served with a glare."

"I told you I'm not a model."

"And I told you that you just had to smile."

"And I told you that I *am* smiling!"

Duncan heard Peter muttering in the corner and saw Clara glancing over there. He lowered the camera. "Out. All of you, out. Thank you. We've got this."

Peter shrugged and left. Emily, who always served as his assistant during shoots, started to protest, but Duncan shook his head. "Please, Emily."

When she'd left, taking the makeup artist, the designer whose clothes Clara was modeling and the rest of the entourage with her, Duncan looked at Clara. "Okay, it's just you and me. We've done this before. No one to feel awkward around. So can I get a smile, please? You can hate me all you want later, I promise."

The grimace and the glare had disappeared, but the smile took a few seconds to break through. "Thank you, I appreciate you doing that. I'll smile, but it's still awkward."

"Do you remember that little black-haired girl in the red dress on Bali who danced on the beach while the other kids fished on the rocks?" he asked.

That made her smile for real. "Yes, she was adorable."

He snapped a series of pictures. "Remember how you danced with her, making her light up with the most beautiful smile? I took pictures, and they're some of the best pictures I've ever taken. Hand at your side, please. Fantastic. I bet that little girl still has the scarf you gave her, probably dancing on the street wearing it right now."

Snapping a few more pictures, he lowered the camera. "Great. Now the next outfit, please."

The look on Clara's face told him she hadn't even realized what he'd done. It made him laugh.

"Sneaky, Duncan. Very sneaky."

"Whatever works, baby."

It did work. By the fourth outfit, he didn't even have to dig for more Bali memories to make her smile and act naturally. The photos were everything he had hoped for. He was grateful that the original model hadn't shown up. Not only had he spent an enjoyable afternoon with Clara and his camera, but no model could have done a better job than Clara once they'd gotten past her initial awkwardness. She was every bit as photogenic as Rachel. Maybe more if he was allowed to be biased.

"Thank you so much, Clara," he said when he'd taken the last photo. "You're a lifesaver."

"You're welcome." She took off the coat she'd been modeling. "I'm really glad I've never been one of those girls dreaming of becoming a model, though. I'd be more comfortable behind the camera."

"That could be arranged, you know. But you were great today. Just wait until you see the final result."

She wrinkled her nose. "I'd rather play with one of your cameras."

"Be my guest, as long as you don't break anything." He started clearing the workspace as Emily and the others came back in. "How about dinner tonight? The town may look dead now that the tourists are gone, but there are a couple of nice restaurants down by the water that are still open."

When she didn't reply, he looked up from what he was doing and saw her having some kind of internal debate. He tried not to take it personally, but he was relieved when she finally smiled. "I'd like that."

"Great. I'll finish up here while you get changed."

It wasn't that easy though. Duncan wasn't the only one who had seen how great Clara was once she'd relaxed. He should have known that Emily had lurked behind the decorative screens at the back of the room where the other door was, but apparently, the designer had been with her. He fawned over Clara and spouted an impressive series of adjectives.

Duncan had everything cleaned up before Clara managed to escape the designer and change into her own clothes.

"I don't think I've ever met anyone who liked the sound of his own voice more than that Lawrence guy," she told Duncan. "He wouldn't let me leave without accepting a piece of the clothing I wore on the photos, no matter how much I protested. Is it okay to accept it?"

Duncan locked the door and led Clara to his car. "Sure, that's normal. Here's your check. It's what I would have paid the model who canceled, but since you don't have a work permit, we'll just do it this way."

"Won't that get you in trouble?"

"Nah. The photos aren't for a magazine or anything. They're for the designer to show people. He could have taken them himself and used his wife or sister as a model. Most do, he said. No one will get in trouble."

She handed him back the envelope with the check. "I don't feel right accepting money for it, Duncan. Can't we just say that I did you a favor and got a fancy, new top for it?"

"You worked for that money," he said seriously. "Please take it."

She let her arm fall. "Thank you."

The expression on her face was unreadable, but she didn't look happy. Duncan reached for her hand. "Hey, at least you can add *model* to your resume now."

"Better than nothing I suppose." Her smile looked a little strained. "Sorry for sounding ungrateful. It's a touchy subject."

When they reached the car, he held the passenger door open for her. "Which subject exactly? Money or your resume?" he asked when he'd gotten into the car himself.

"Both." She sighed. "I turned down a college fund and inheritances from unknown grandparents. I think I offended Mr. and Mrs. Quinn, but I just couldn't take it."

"I can't blame you. I didn't think I deserved my college fund either." He wanted to ask why her resume was a touchy subject, but he didn't. There were times when Clara looked exhausted. He suspected it had to do with still being overwhelmed with the new reality of her life. He just wanted to make her smile and forget whatever weighed her down.

"Let's forget about touchy subjects. What are you in the mood for, seafood or Italian? I'm afraid those are the best options unless you want a pizza or a burger."

"Get me a burger and you'll be my favorite person in the whole world."

Duncan grinned. "My kind of girl."

* * * *

The phone woke Duncan the following morning. Still half asleep, he groped for it on the nightstand until he finally located it.

"'Lo?" he rasped into the receiver.

"You're late, boss."

He opened his eyes. "Emily?"

"Bingo. Will we be seeing you anytime soon?"

"What time is it?" He sat up and squinted at the alarm clock.

"It's just after nine and your first appointment of the day just arrived. Want me to handle it?"

Rubbing his forehead, he sighed. "Yes. Thanks."

"Christmas bonus will be big this year, huh boss?" She was laughing when she hung up.

Duncan shook his head and dragged himself into the shower. He needed to wake up, and he needed to wake up fast. The dream that apparently made him sleep through the alarm had been steamy and full of Clara. If he didn't push it to the back of his mind, he'd get nothing accomplished all day.

Dinner the previous night had been great. Clara was a very uncomplicated woman when she wasn't caught up in her head and trying to give more of herself than she could to her new family. They'd had a lot of fun. So much fun, it seemed that she was more stuck on his mind than usual.

It was late when Duncan finally plopped down in his office chair. He always checked his work e-mail and his schedule for the next day before going home. In his inbox, he found an interesting e-mail. It was an assignment offer from a guy at a magazine he'd done some work for in the past. The good thing was it was in New York and would pay well.

The bad part was that it was just a few days away.

He leaned back in his chair. He did out of town assignments regularly. Sometimes far away like Bali, sometimes just across the state border. He'd always enjoyed them, too. But nowhere inside of him did he have a desire to leave Connecticut, even if it was just for a few days. Although he'd been too chicken to ask, he knew that Clara wouldn't stay forever. She had a life in Denmark. He didn't want to waste time by going out of town while she was in the same place he was. He'd already been without her too long.

Sighing, he realized he was being pathetic. He had a career to worry about. He needed to make smart decisions. Going to New York for a few days would be smart. Clara would still be in Stonebridge when he returned. At least, he hoped she would be.

Before he could talk himself out of it, he replied to the e-mail and accepted the assignment. He'd almost made it to his car before he regretted it. However, by the time he parked outside the local pizza place, he'd come up with a fantastic plan of how to make it a good trip after all.

It wasn't unusual for Duncan to show up at Luke's place with takeout after work, but he was really there to see Clara.

"Great, I'm starving," Luke greeted him and grabbed the pizza boxes when Duncan walked through the door.

"Ever heard of cooking?" Duncan asked.

"Clara said she'd cook, but then she started painting. That was several hours ago."

"You're so pathetic. Where is she?"

Luke had already started stuffing his face with pizza, so he just pointed down the hall.

Duncan went down there and found the guest bedroom door slightly ajar. He watched from the door as Clara, with her back turned, captured the very essence of Rachel on her canvas. Her talent was extraordinary. Duncan didn't need a degree in art to see that.

He knocked on the door. "Am I interrupting?"

Clara turned around so fast it almost looked like a pirouette. "No, of course not. Hi."

"Hi, yourself. Your talent is kind of mind-blowing, you know. I originally became fascinated with photography because it captures moments in time in a way I believed nothing else could. I might be wrong."

She shrugged. "It's difficult to capture one single moment unless you have a photographic memory, a photograph or someone willing to stand very still for a very, very long moment."

"Take the compliment, Clara."

She laughed. "Thank you."

"Luke says you're starving him."

"What?" Clara looked at her wristwatch. "Oh! I'd lost track of the time. I said I'd cook."

"I brought pizza. That should keep him busy for a moment. I wanted to talk to you." Duncan watched as she straightened her back, almost as if she expected bad news.

"I just took an assignment in New York. I'll be there for at least three days. Come with me."

"Come with you to New York?" She kept wiping her hands in a paint-spotted kitchen towel. "Are you sure that's a good idea?"

"It's an excellent idea, baby. Best one I've had in ages."

"Duncan…"

"Clara. Come on. It will be fun. I'll show you New York. You've only seen bits and pieces of Connecticut. It's time to broaden your American horizon."

"You know, I only came here to connect with my family. Not to sightsee."

"You've connected with your family and you're still here," he pointed out. "Besides, when you planned to come here, you didn't know I'd be here. Come on. What if I say please?"

She smiled but still looked pensive. Absentmindedly, she wiped a hand across her forehead, leaving a little smudge of green paint behind. He wanted to snap a picture of her with his phone but figured he needed to behave if he wanted her to say yes.

"Look at it this way then. Free trip to New York, personal tour guide, a few days without Quinns bombing your mind and since it's you; I'll throw in a couple of photography lessons."

"Okay, I'll be honest. I'd love to go to New York with you. I've always wanted to go there. Plus, I'd love to spend time with you. But we need rules. There can't be any kissing or anything. I've already stayed in America longer than I intended. Leaving will just be harder if you and I... You know what I mean."

"Yeah, I know what you mean." He leaned back against the doorframe and crossed his arms. "But I don't like your rules."

Chapter Twelve

"What's wrong with my rules? They're very sensible." Clara resisted the urge to wipe her hands on the dirty rag again. They weren't going to get clean until she washed them, and she recognized a nervous habit when she saw one.

"Exactly. Sensible. We don't need sensible. There's no fun in sensible."

The look in his eyes scared and excited her at the same time. "Duncan…"

"You know, when you say my name like that, you're breaking my heart." He took a step closer to her. "You know what else? I bet if I kissed you right now, you'd change your mind about those rules."

"There's another option. If you kissed me right now, you could also end up covered in paint."

He shrugged. "I'll risk it."

Clara could have protested. She could have resisted and stopped him. Instead, she melted into his arms and let him claim her lips for a moment before being sucked in by the passion that seemed to always be present when she was around him.

"Awkward."

Clara pulled away from Duncan, feeling a little lightheaded. She saw Luke wrinkling his nose in the doorway.

"Go away, man," Duncan told him.

"What? It's my house." Luke took a bite of a pizza slice. "Can I just say that I take back every time I've ever felt bad about being so overprotective of Rachel that she hardly ever dated? Seeing your sister kissing someone like that is just wrong."

"Then go away," Duncan repeated impatiently.

Clara hid her face in Duncan's shirt to muffle her laughter. He pulled her closer and chuckled into her hair. "Luke. Go eat your pizza."

"I'm leaving the door open."

"Jesus Christ," Duncan muttered.

Clara took a step back when Luke had left. The moment was gone and with it whatever had clouded her mind. "I was always taught not to play with fire, but this one time when I was around ten, I did it anyway because I was so fascinated by the flames. I burned my curtains and most of the bedding on my bed. I feel like I'm ten again, only this time I know the risk."

Duncan grinned, obviously taking it as a compliment. She wasn't sure she'd meant it as one. Fighting something she just wanted to give into was tiring, but the prospect of a broken heart scared her.

"So... About those rules?"

"You fight dirty," she told him.

"Never claimed I didn't, baby. If I have to, I'll use all my tricks to lure out the Clara from Bali who didn't hold back so much. I liked her a lot."

"Tricks?" She sighed tiredly. That was exactly what she needed. *Tricks.* "New rule to replace the others. No tricks."

"Okay," he agreed easily. "No tricks. I don't need tricks."

Clara shook her head. *Could you deflate a guy's ego with something sharp and pointy?* How was it possible to want and fear something so much at the same time? There were times when the wanting part overpowered her, but other times, the instinct to flee was stronger. Such as right then.

"I have to go cook. I promised Luke," she said, brushing him off. Then she swallowed a sigh as she heard her own words. "Stay for dinner?"

Duncan suddenly looked as pensive as Clara felt. "Yeah. Thanks."

Mustering a small smile, Clara fled as gracefully as she could. She had no idea why her brain was all over the place, but maybe a little time-out alone in the kitchen would help.

She listened to Luke and Duncan talk in the living room while she cooked. Luke was arguing that the pizzas Duncan had brought were merely a snack. Any other time, it would have made her laugh, but there was no time for laughing when you were busy analyzing yourself.

Luke was the perfect buffer while they ate. Well, except for the looks he kept sending both her and Duncan. She wasn't an expert on brothers, so she'd have to ask Rachel if they always poked their noses in stuff that didn't concern them. She had a feeling they did.

While the manly men discussed football, Clara spent most of the meal considering what was becoming more and more of a problem— Duncan. She was in love with him. The ache in her heart when she'd realized that he wasn't going to call had told her that. Moreover, the ache in her heart now when she thought about going back home, told her the same thing.

The problem was she couldn't see herself fitting in if she stayed in Connecticut. As much as she bonded with everyone, she was still an outsider. Besides, how do you just leave your entire life and move halfway around the world? Clara had been overwhelmed when she'd moved half an hour away from the home in which she'd been raised. Moving to another continent… She couldn't even wrap her mind around it.

Even though she'd extended her stay, she would eventually go home. A relationship didn't fit into that plan. Not a real relationship anyway. So she was stuck between wanting Duncan and trying to keep him at arm's length. It would be hard enough to leave as it was, making it worse was just stupid.

"Earth to Clara!"

"What?" She looked up to see Luke trying not to laugh.

"Are you okay?" he asked.

She nodded. "Yeah. Just thinking."

"Heavy thoughts by the looks of it," Duncan commented, not as amused as Luke.

Forcing herself to smile, she shrugged it off. Even though cocky, confident Duncan was a handful, she preferred him to the somber version across the table. "Just lost in thought."

"Glad you got unlost." Duncan sent her a quick smile and continued eating.

A smile tugged at the corners of her lips. Maybe she just needed to relax and stop thinking so much. Duncan had shown on several occasions that even though he was eager to try to change her mind about holding back, he respected her boundaries. Kind of, anyway.

Luke cleared his throat. "As I was saying... Crap. Now I've forgotten what I was saying."

"Senile," Duncan commented as Clara laughed.

Her cell phone rang and she excused herself as the guys kept bantering about who was more senile. Perhaps *juvenile* was a better term for it, she wondered as she picked up Rachel's call.

"Are you free tomorrow? Mom and I are testing out cake recipes for her new cookbook. Well, *she* is. I'll probably just be in the way with my cast and eat all the frosting since that's exactly what my thighs need. Join us?"

Clara laughed. Rachel was a true sister. Resisting frosting was impossible. "Sure, I'd love to. When?"

"Awesome. Come by around nine. Dad promised he'd lure Aunt Tilda out of the house somehow. She's off on another cruise in a few days, so she probably needs to shop or something. The last thing we need is her advice, well-meant or not."

"All right. I'll see you tomorrow then."

Clara was smiling when she ended the call. Sometimes at night when she closed her eyes, she could still hear the sound of the car hitting Rachel, so having the old Rachel back was such a relief. Trying to bond a little more with her parents had also been on her agenda for a while, but she'd had a difficult time figuring out how. Maybe baking was the answer when it came to Grace Quinn.

After helping to clean up after dinner, Duncan said he had to go catch up on some work. "Is New York a go?" he asked Clara, as he was putting on his jacket.

Having almost forgotten about his offer after the kiss and Rachel's call, Clara inhaled sharply. The urge to give into the fear was there, but refusing was not an option. She wanted to go with him. Not just to see New York, a place that had been on her top ten list of places to visit for years, but to spend time with him. Maybe she had it all wrong. Maybe she was wasting precious time pushing him away—time she could spend having a good time instead.

"It's a go. Thank you for asking me." Her smile was genuine as she silently swore to banish all doubt and fear of heartache from her mind.

His smile was wide, a little smug and impossibly sexy. "I really, really want to kiss you, but last time I did, I nearly lost you to your heavy thoughts."

"There's a lesson in there somewhere," she teased.

He sighed theatrically and placed a hand over his heart. "Naughty schoolteacher fantasy right there. Teach me anything you'd like."

"Fucking hell. That's my sister! Who are you, man? Get out of my house!" Luke, the not-so-stealthy eavesdropper, yelled from behind the half-closed door to the living room.

Clara and Duncan laughed. "It's like high school all over again," he said. "Trying to get a kiss on the front porch without being interrupted by the parents. I find myself a lot less intimidated now. I can totally take Luke."

At her unimpressed look, he grinned. "All right, I'm off. If I don't see you before Thursday, be ready to go just after lunch, okay? I'll pick you up here."

"Okay. I'll be ready."

He smiled and leaned in for the kiss she'd been telling herself that she hadn't been hoping for. His lips claimed hers, coaxing her to forget the world around her. It was a quick surrender.

She had no idea how long the kiss lasted when he pulled back. "Goodnight, Clara."

"Goodnight." It wasn't until she'd watched him get into his car that she realized the high school remark before was very much valid. She was acting like a lovesick teenager. She winced as she slammed the door shut with a little more force than necessary. No more thoughts of Duncan Cantwell that night.

After calming herself and her quick-beating heart down, she went into her room to grab Luke's journal, along with one she'd been writing in herself. In the living room, she plopped down on the couch next to Luke.

"You're a brat," she informed him.

"And you're my sister. Sisters shouldn't be allowed to kiss or date or have sex. Someone really should have made this a law centuries ago."

"If this law of yours had been in effect for centuries, you would never have been born. No one would."

"Sisters also shouldn't make so much sense. It's annoying." He grinned at her. "But apart from that, I'm happy for you. He makes you smile."

Biting the inside of her cheek to keep from smiling goofily, she looked away. "Not going there."

"Thank God."

Shaking her head, she handed him his journal. "I'm sorry I've taken so long to read it and talk to you about it. I just wanted to give you some solid, or as solid as it comes, proof that you're not crazy. Well, at least you're not the only one who's crazy."

"This…" She looked down at the notebook in her hands. "I don't have a photographic memory or anything, but I've been trying to remember if I've ever felt anything like you have—unexplained feelings that couldn't be chalked up to something that was happening in my life. I have. I just thought it was either normal or that I was weird. I've written some of it down as I remember it. I've also commented on yours."

She looked up at him. "Everything in your journal hit home. It kind of freaked me out at first, because how do you explain something like that? You felt what I felt all these years. I don't want to end up on the cover of some magazine as half of the wonder twins because you got depressed when my parents died."

"I've taken enough abuse because of it already," Luke replied. "I've never told anyone the details before. I just… We have this connection. *We* do. It's no one else's business. I don't even know if it's there now."

"What do you mean?"

He shrugged. "I could feel you were close that day you came here. But since? Nothing. I mean, I pick up on you being confused and overwhelmed, but it shows on your face, you know. I don't know. Maybe it was because we were apart."

Clara rubbed two fingers against each temple and closed her eyes briefly. "That sounds freakier than what I read in your journal."

"I'm sorry. My point is that the connection is there. Truthfully, if it hadn't been, I don't know if I'd been able to keep the hope alive all those years."

"Then thank God for unexplainable twin connections." She raised an imaginary glass as if to toast him and smiled. Then she gave him her own notebook. "Here. That's for you."

He looked at it for a long time. "Thank you."

"Happy reading. I'm going to head to bed. Big baking day at the Quinn House tomorrow."

"Really? Sounds like I need to swing by." He grinned. "Duncan will be there for sure. He has a sixth sense when it comes to cakes. It's freakier than any twin connection you could possibly imagine."

Clara laughed and rose from the couch. "I'll barricade the door. Goodnight, Luke."

"Night, sis."

Sis. The word never failed to make her smile, but it wasn't sisterly things she was thinking about as she drifted off to sleep. It was thoughts of Duncan.

* * * *

The next day started out well enough. Clara went for a run before heading over to the Quinn House for a day of baking. On the walk there, she talked to Danny on the phone, discussing the weekend's Danish soccer results. Not that Clara particularly cared about them, but it seemed to make Danny happy that she took an interest in it. It was *their* thing because no one else in the family knew about Danish soccer. Clara thought it was cute that he still took an interest in his old club.

"Good morning, dear." Grace Quinn was, as always, impeccably dressed and already wearing her usual apron. Clara briefly wondered how many memories the Quinn kids had of her *not* wearing an apron. She didn't think it was a lot.

"Good morning…Grace." It was the first time she called the woman who had given birth to her anything but Mrs. Quinn. At first, it had been the only label Clara was willing to consider but lately it had started to sound wrong. *Feel* wrong.

Judging by the smile that lit up Grace's face, the title change was appreciated. Clara returned the smile and stepped inside.

"Carl took Aunt Tilda over to check on her house today," Grace told her. "I love the woman, but she does stick her nose in everything. She loves commenting on people's cooking, giving them advice but the truth is, she hasn't cooked a meal in more than thirty years."

"I'm sure the world is full of people who don't cook," Clara said, straight-faced.

Grace laughed and pushed the door to the kitchen open. "She would say that."

Rachel greeted Clara enthusiastically. She looked like her old self. The bruises had faded. A slightly different hairdo covered the healing wound on her forehead. The only outward sign of her accident was the cast on her wrist, and it wasn't enough to slow her down. A few days after being released from the hospital, she'd made Clara paint brightly colored flowers on it.

Clara and Rachel were both given a handwritten recipe and set to work. Apparently, Grace wrote down recipes all the time. They would pile up until she had a chance to test them out. Rachel often helped her out, although she claimed that she wasn't a very good cook.

"My head is full of other things, and then I forget what I'm doing. I can't count the times I've burned something because I got distracted. Oops," she told Clara while vigorously whipping the batter to some kind of cake.

"I've been meaning to ask you, Clara. Would you be willing to part with the recipe for the chocolate cake you made for Duncan's birthday?" Grace asked. "It was spectacular."

Clara laughed. "I found something online for inspiration and then just winged it since the birthday boy wanted everything to be chocolate."

"Oh." Grace laughed with her. "I thought it might be a secret family recipe or something."

"Not at all." Clara grabbed a pencil and looked around for some paper. "I'll just write it down. I think I remember it pretty accurately, but you might have to test it again."

Finding a notebook, she sat down at the breakfast table and wrote down the recipe. When she was satisfied that she'd gotten everything down, she handed it to Grace. "We can always claim it's a secret family recipe."

"It's enticing enough as it is, but an interesting story never hurts," Grace agreed. "We can call it 'Eve'—sorry—'Clara's Chocolate Dream'."

Clara chose to ignore the 'Eve,' though she'd thought they were past that. "'Duncan's Chocolate Dream' is probably more appropriate. I wanted to go in a completely different direction, but the man is very determined when it comes to chocolate, isn't he?"

"Understatement of the year," Rachel commented dryly. "He throws tantrums over chocolate."

"I remember a certain teenage girl who threw tantrums whenever I served meat for dinner," Grace pointed out, defending Duncan like a mama bear. "That was during your vegetarian phase."

"That was totally different." Rachel stuck a finger in the cake batter to taste it. "That was political."

Clara chuckled at the banter as she continued with her own cake recipe. It was an apple and blueberry cake that reminded her of one her grandmother used to make with marzipan and raisins instead. Everything was different and still the same.

Engrossed in what she was doing and not wanting to mess anything up, Clara barely noticed Grace stepping out to take a phone call. A little later, when she heard her biological mom's voice drifting in through the half-open kitchen door, she took notice, though.

"We have our Eve back. Well, it's still so new and all, but I'm sure she'll get used to being Eve Quinn soon, even though she was raised as someone else," Clara heard Grace say. "I know. I almost can't believe it! It's a long story. I'll tell you all about it when we meet for lunch."

Behind Clara, Rachel cleared her throat, but Clara turned back to her cake. It was like a punch in the stomach or a bucket of cold water in the face to hear Grace talk like that. Clara thought they'd gotten further than that. It was disappointing to realize her own mother didn't have it in her to accept her daughter the way she was. Clara had no intentions of changing for anyone.

Not in the mood to argue or try to solve the seemingly unsolvable riddle that was her new parents, she let her thoughts drift to her upcoming trip to New York with the chocolate monster instead. Even to herself, she was reluctant to admit how excited she was about it. New York City. With Duncan.

As if Rachel had read her mind, she bumped her hip against Clara's. "Saturday night. Bar hopping in New London. What do you say? We're young, free and single. Life's not going to wait for us. We gotta catch up, sister!"

Eyebrows raised, Clara tried not to laugh. "What's in that cake batter?"

Rachel shrugged. "Come on. Live a little!"

"I'm sorry. I can't this weekend. Duncan thought I needed to... broaden my American horizon, I think he called it. I'm tagging along when he heads to New York on an assignment."

"Come again? You're going to New York with Duncan when he's working?" Rachel asked.

"Yes." Clara was pretty sure it sounded innocent enough.

"Duncan doesn't like people hanging around when he works. I should know since I bug him every time he gets an assignment somewhere exotic. How did you talk him into it?"

Clara sighed inwardly and made a mental note that kicking Duncan's ass was on the agenda when she saw him next. "He invited me."

Rachel's eyes widened. "That rotten... Ugh! I'm gonna break his teeth so he can't eat another piece of chocolate."

"I'm sorry. I had no idea." Clara wished she hadn't stepped right into the middle of a conflict she hadn't even been aware existed. Who knew having siblings was so complicated?

"Oh no, don't you dare apologize." Rachel chuckled and shook her head. "That boy is going to regret ever denying me when I wanted to go to Iceland. To Argentina. To Bali. To friggin' Australia!"

Grace's cough made Rachel stop her little tirade. "What?" she asked her mom.

"I, for one am happy that you didn't go to Bali," Grace replied, having come back to the kitchen without Clara noticing. The older woman looked meaningfully at Clara. "That was where Clara and Duncan met."

Chapter Thirteen

Duncan had always figured that if World War III ever started, he'd hear about it on the news first, not walk right into it when entering his childhood home.

A spatula hit the door right above his head when he took his first step into the kitchen. Rachel came right at him. "Why the hell didn't you tell me?" she demanded. She hit his shoulder with her good hand before laughing. "You crazy kids."

He looked at her, wondering if she was aware that she looked as crazy as she sounded. She had flour in her hair, cake batter on her cheek and the insane laughing was worrying him. "Are you okay?"

"Am I okay?" She laughed again. "Am I okay? Why yes, Duncan. I'm just fine. I was busy experiencing my first small episode of sisterly jealousy when Mom told me I had no reason to. Because apparently I was the only one you didn't tell that you already knew Clara when she came here. What the hell, Duncan?"

World War threat averted. Sisterly tantrum not so much. He glanced at Clara, who bit her lip to kill a smile before turning back to whatever she was doing at the kitchen table. "Power down, woman. Hello, ladies."

Rachel hit him again.

"Would you stop that? Jesus Christ." He rubbed his arm and stepped away from her. "It's not like I've told everyone but you that I knew Clara before, so simmer the hell down before I get annoyed."

"Don't tell me what to do!"

"All right then. Act like a spoiled brat if you must."

She huffed and puffed for a bit before finally letting out a sigh. "You could have told me. That goes for both of you, by the way, but especially you, Duncan."

"I'm sorry," Clara said quietly without turning around.

"Don't apologize, Clara." Duncan narrowed his eyes playfully at Rachel. "It's not like this one is usually in a big rush to share who she goes out with or anything."

Rachel gasped. "What? You went out? Dammit, what else haven't you told me?"

Duncan laughed, pleased that he could answer her question truthfully without feeding her curiosity further. "No, we didn't go out." He was pretty sure he saw Clara shake. He hoped it was from suppressed laughter and not something else.

"You need to send out newsletters or something." Rachel blew out a breath. "This is huge and I didn't even know."

"Poor deprived Rachel. Now I smell cake and I see cake. When will I be tasting cake?"

"Yeah, like you'll be getting cake." Rachel snorted and crossed her arms, awkwardly because of the cast. "Why am I never allowed to go with you on assignments?"

"Because you're a brat. Christ, Rach. I want to show Clara more of the country than just Stonebridge."

"You could have shown me Australia."

Duncan rolled his eyes. "Were you born in Australia?"

"Ugh. Stop being so rational. You make me sound even more irrational than I am."

"Stop it, both of you." Mama Q handed Duncan a plate with cake and pointed to the kitchen table. "Sit. Don't talk. Rachel, I believe you were in the middle of a recipe. It's like you're teenagers again."

Duncan did as instructed. He didn't mind. Cake and Rachel shutting up was the perfect endgame. He caught Clara smiling as she kept working on whatever it was she was so busy with. Rachel, on the other hand, poked her tongue out at him. He just smirked and ate his cake.

It was true that she'd bugged him to come with him on assignments almost as long as he'd taken them. And he'd been honest when he'd told her he didn't like people breathing down his neck when he worked. It just hadn't occurred to him at all when he'd asked Clara to New York. Not that he was worried she'd annoy him or anything, but he hadn't even considered the possibility. It probably wasn't something he should ever mention to Rachel.

"So, what's in New York that requires you and your camera?" Mama Q asked him. She was at the stove, stirring something in a pan.

"It's a travel thing. I've done some stuff for the magazine before. They're doing a feature with green oases in major cities. Not the most interesting thing in the world, but I like the magazine and New York is hard to pass up. The change of pace for a few days will be good."

"That's nice. Rachel, maybe we should go to New York to do our Christmas shopping this year? You, too, Clara, if you want to come. We could make a trip of it and pamper ourselves for a few days."

"I'm game. Since Duncan doesn't want to take me and all." Rachel narrowed her eyes at him, which he rewarded with a quick grin. His real interest was in Clara, though. He didn't know how long she was planning to stay in America, but he'd heard her avoid the subject of Christmas once when talking to Linda, so he doubted she'd be around that long. He was in no rush for the holidays to come.

"Um...we'll see." Clara smiled to disarm what was probably a refusal.

Shifting his gaze to Rachel and Mama Q, there were no signs on their faces that they'd heard it as anything but a *maybe*. Had they conveniently forgotten that Clara had a life somewhere else? If so, he wished he had their memory. He was having a hard time blocking it out.

* * * *

Duncan was in a great mood when he drove down I-95 Thursday afternoon. Clara was sitting next to him, although she hadn't looked at him since they'd left Stonebridge behind. For someone who hadn't seemed particularly interested in going when he'd first asked her, she had yet to stop staring out the window. It wasn't even the most interesting scenery.

"Is Denmark very different than here?" he asked.

She turned her head to look at him. "Actually, I was just thinking that the fall colors are a lot like they are at home. So pretty. The climate in this part of the country is a lot like the Danish, too. Other than that... Yeah, it's different. The people, the vastness of the land, the grocery stores."

He chuckled. "Still not getting friendly with the canned goods,

106

huh?"

"No." She was able to squeeze so much disgust into the little, two-letter word.

Conversation flowed easily the entire ride, but he wasn't unaware of her effect on him. Being trapped inside the car with her for so long was exhilarating and maddening at the same time.

He'd booked them rooms at a not too shabby hotel located close enough for them to be able to walk to Central Park where his job was located for a few days. He'd lied and told her that the magazine was footing the bill, knowing it was easier than getting her to accept that he was paying.

They had dinner at a Thai restaurant at Clara's insistence, and then they called it a night, as Duncan had to be up early so he could capture what he hoped, prayed and begged the deities would be a spectacular sunrise.

It was chilly the following morning, but Clara didn't complain as she tagged along, warming her hands on a cup of coffee. She had a self-proclaimed love affair with Starbucks and had, half-asleep, wondered if she could take a Starbucks shop home with her and place it on the nearest street corner.

Duncan had always enjoyed being right. While trying to make Central Park look as alluring as possible, he realized he'd been right never to let Rachel or anyone else tag along on assignments before. It was distracting to have Clara around while trying to work. He hadn't felt it on Bali because he'd pretty much gotten what he had needed before seeing her on the beach. But this time, he felt her presence constantly, even if she was doing her best not to be in his way.

She had borrowed one of his cameras and flittered around taking pictures of God knew what. He had a feeling that whatever motifs she found, he'd get a unique peek into her mind when he saw the pictures later. That distracted him too much. The usual ease he experienced when picking up a camera was gone.

"This place is amazing," Clara gushed when they were eating lunch. He'd wanted to take her somewhere nice, but she'd insisted on staying in Central Park and having hotdogs as that made her feel right at home.

Duncan was no stranger to New York City where he'd gone to

college and Central Park where he'd spent quite a few mornings running. However, he'd never seen it through Clara's eyes before. It fascinated him to hear what she thought of everything.

"It's like... Well, actually I don't know what it's like. The biggest park I've ever seen is Phoenix Park in Dublin, but it's nothing like this. It's so full of life here," she continued and looked at him with a wide smile. "Not difficult to find something to take pictures of. I've decided that I envy you your career. You don't get as messy when you take a picture as when you paint one. Plus it's so much faster."

The late fall wind rustled Clara's hair, making her look adorably rumpled. He smiled when she impatiently brushed it away from her face. Vain she was not. "It's easier to learn how to take pictures than it is to paint them," he pointed out. "Besides, you can paint stuff that only exists in your head. I have to make do with reality."

"There is that, I suppose. You know, Luke asked me if the Bali beach I gave you only existed in my head."

"And what did you tell him?"

"The truth. Then it escalated into something that I remembered too late isn't something you discuss with your brother."

Duncan grinned. "Oh, really?"

"Not that, you pervert." She shook her head, unable to fight the smile off completely. "But he assured me he'd heard worse from Rachel."

"Yeah, we all have. Awkward. But he's the only one who the parental unit thought was gay because of it."

"He mentioned that," she said, giggling. "I'm sensing a really interesting story there."

"If you tell Luke I told you, I'll deny it," Duncan warned her. "But it was when Rachel had just discovered that boys were interesting and not just gross. Her best friend moved away. You know how girls that age are; they need someone to gossip with. So she chose Luke, who was... Well, he was going through a rough phase at school. A teenage boy *sensing* his sister whom everyone except our family presumed dead, wasn't a real hit with his classmates. So Rachel latched on and Luke let her. She would talk about boys constantly, which made Mama and Papa Q think that he'd taken an interest in boys, too."

He chuckled. "They were very cool about it, but Luke was mortified when they tried to talk to him. Ben, Danny and I weren't too nice. Teenage boys, you know."

"Poor Luke. So it's kind of my fault."

"It's completely your fault. Assuming that your baby self ordered the kidnapping." He rolled his eyes. "Don't be stupid, Clara."

She sighed. "When I hear about what Luke's been through because of the connection he had with me, it's hard not to feel a little guilty. He was defending me in a way."

"And he'd do it all over again in a heartbeat."

"Damn Quinns," she muttered.

"Amen," he agreed, laughing. "So, are you ready to leave? We've got places to go and stuff to see."

Duncan showed Clara some of the typical tourist stuff in New York, but he wasn't overly surprised when she expressed interest in something less typical.

"Can we go to Ellis Island? My great-grandmother's brother and sister came through there. My grandmother always told me about their letters before she died. She only saw them once or twice in her life, but they wrote letters regularly."

"Sure," Duncan agreed easily. He didn't care where they went as long as it made Clara happy. "Do you have family here then?"

She shook her head. "It was never said aloud, probably because it wasn't something you talked about back then, but I think my great-grandmother's brother was gay. Some of the stuff my grandmother told me... It just fits. His sister kept house for him and never married either."

After Ellis Island, they went in search of art galleries. The more hidden on some back street the better, as far as Clara was concerned. Duncan followed gladly, discovering that he was having a great time.

"I think you should consider taking Rachel along with you sometime," Clara told him over dinner. They had found a restaurant promising Nordic cuisine and Clara, being the expert and all, claimed it delivered what it promised.

"Rachel throws tantrums. It's her thing," he pointed out.

"Maybe. But look at it from her point of view. You tell her no all the time, and then you invite me the first chance you get."

She had a point, but he hated having to admit it. "I'll think about it."

"You should invite her before she gets a chance to ask again."

The impish smile on Clara's face made Duncan laugh. "Yes, dear."

"Ass."

"You like my ass."

"Actually, you're the one obsessed with your own ass. I should have studied psychology."

Their banter turned flirtier over dessert. Duncan saw the Clara from Bali reappear in all her radiant and carefree glory. He hadn't even realized how much had been missing. Clearly, the whole Quinn business was still weighing heavily on her.

He grabbed her hand when they left the restaurant. It was dark and the streets were crowded, which would have been his excuse if she'd protested. But she didn't.

"Thank you for inviting me along," she said instead. "I'm sorry I made a fuss about it. It's a great place. I'm having a wonderful time."

"I'm glad." He squeezed her hand and smiled into the night. Sometimes life was just the right kind of awesome.

Chapter Fourteen

Clara woke up dizzy and nauseous. Even before she opened her eyes, the world was spinning madly, and she grabbed a handful of the bedding, trying to anchor herself. She didn't remember where she was or what she'd been doing, but if she had to make a bet, her money would be on alcohol somehow being involved.

Awareness started to seep in at the same time as the splitting headache. *New York. Duncan. A dimly lit bar. Vodka. Letting go of everything that had been holding her back. Oh no...*

She opened her eyes. The first thing she saw was Duncan coming out from the bathroom wearing jeans and a towel around his neck.

"Morning, sleepyhead."

Trying to speak only made her cough, so she reached for the glass of water on the bedside table before trying again. "What are you doing in my room?"

Duncan plopped down on the edge of the bed. "The correct question is 'what are you doing in *my* room?'"

Clara looked around. Damn. He was right. "Okay, what am I doing in your room?"

That made him laugh. He threw the towel on the floor as he stood up to go find a shirt. "You don't remember?"

"If I remembered, I wouldn't ask, would I?"

"Honestly, I've given up trying to figure out your brain. I tried at first, but it made me want to punch things. I've been much happier since I stopped trying."

She shook her head, but quickly stopped and cradled her face in her hands. Damn headache. "Duncan. If you don't tell me why I'm in your room, I'll vomit on your pillow. Actually, I may do that anyway if I don't like your answer, but please tell me."

111

The mattress wobbled slightly when he sat down again. "Speaking of vomit, you got so drunk last night that I was afraid to leave you alone in case you choked or something."

"Ugh. Is that it?" The smell of coffee made her open her eyes carefully. Duncan was holding a cup out toward her. She gratefully accepted it.

"Should there be more?"

Clara shrugged. "I don't know. That's the problem."

"You got drunk, let go of some inhibitions and then you passed out."

Wincing, she sipped the hot coffee. "Do I want details on the whole inhibitions part?"

He grinned. "Probably not. But I swear, it wasn't bad."

"Tell me."

"You wanted to dance on the table, but I stopped you. You wanted to give me a lap dance, but I stopped you. After a moment. Seriously, Clara, the whole thing made me realize the pressure you've been under lately, trying to fit in and stuff. You were just letting off steam, which you shouldn't be embarrassed about. You were funny."

"Funny…" She sighed and sipped the coffee. Maybe it was a good thing she didn't remember. And he could be lying about the lap dance. Maybe… "I need a shower."

"I'll order breakfast. I need a few more shots at the park before we return home. I was thinki—"

"Where are my clothes?" Clara shrieked—making her head throb even more—when she realized she was only wearing panties under the sheets.

"Foot end of the bed." Duncan pulled out her top to show her. "I woke up with your bra around my ankle. You must have felt hot during the night."

"This morning just keeps getting worse. Now excuse me while I hijack your shower."

She ignored his chuckling and grabbed her clothes. She couldn't face the world before she'd had a shower, not even the few feet to her own room.

Under the hot spray, the fog cleared a little from her brain. She could almost believe she was still human and not just a headachy mess.

Images from the previous night started filling her head, images that didn't match what Duncan had told her.

That bastard.

She hadn't tried to dance on a table. She certainly hadn't attempted to give him a lap dance. Clara slid down the wall and sat on the wet tiles while the water drummed into her scalp. The reality was much, much worse. Would the satisfaction of punching the wall be worth the pain? Clara sighed and admitted to herself that it probably wouldn't. Punching Duncan, however…

The alcohol she'd consumed the previous night had gotten rid of whatever it was that had been holding her back. She'd kissed him thoroughly, nearly mounting him right there at the bar. Maybe that was where his lap dance fantasy originated. He did stop her eventually. The bastard was a gentleman, at least. But the kiss wasn't the bad part. They'd done that before.

All too clearly, Clara remembered how she'd asked Duncan to go with her back to Copenhagen. Begged him in that unattractive way that only drunk people mastered. Perhaps all she ever needed to know about Duncan Cantwell was that he'd made up a 'dancing on the table' and 'lap dance' story to save her from embarrassment. Because she knew he'd said it for her sake. The look on his face when she'd asked had said it all.

He had wanted to say yes.

If only she'd been too drunk to remember it. Of course, it was only fair that she remembered it since Duncan did, too. He'd been just a little buzzed. Moreover, he'd been sweet about the request. He had laughed it off and told her to quit drinking, no doubt, seeing it was the alcohol talking or the alcohol giving her the courage to say the words aloud. If there was a way to make it happen, to fuse two lives across the globe…

"Breakfast is here!"

Clara sniffled and got up from the floor. Somewhere deep inside of her, there was a woman in control of herself. It was just a shame that Clara seemed to have forgotten her in Denmark.

Instead of putting on her clothes from the night before, she grabbed the robe hanging in the bathroom. There was no dress code for breakfast in a hotel room. With nothing to work with, she ran her fingers through her hair and braided it. A look in the mirror confirmed that she didn't look her best, but at least she looked a little better than she felt. Small mercies and all that.

"Remind me never to drink again," she said to Duncan as she plopped down in one of the chairs around the small table where he'd laid out their meal.

"You know that doesn't work, right?"

"Yeah." She sighed and eyed the pancakes. The thought of something sweet made her nauseous. She needed salty. "Can I have your bacon?"

He looked almost offended. "What? No way. Eat your own."

"You can have my pancakes."

"I don't want your pancakes."

Grabbing a plate with what was apparently her half of the bacon, she had to smile. So Duncan was a bacon-hogging bastard, but he never failed to make her smile. "Thanks."

"For what?" His eyes narrowed. He practically hugged his plate as if still expecting her to steal his bacon.

"For letting me blow off steam last night. It all came to me while I was showering. I appreciate what you did. And tried to do."

"Oh. Well..." He shrugged. "I figured I could at least try."

Clara nodded. "Thank you."

* * * *

Duncan headed back to Central Park after breakfast and Clara went to her own room. After dressing, she curled up on the bed and turned on the TV, hoping mindless noise could tune out her thoughts. When it didn't work, she texted a little with Luke and Rachel instead.

Her headache was fading, making her more lucid thoughts turn, as they often did, to Duncan. *Duncan, Duncan, Duncan.* If she had thought she'd been smitten after Bali, it was nothing compared to how she felt after having spent time with him and gotten to know him better. Love was beautiful and hurt like a bitch.

Before she even realized so much time had passed, he was knocking on her door, carrying lunch.

"Hey. I didn't know if you were up to going out, so I got takeaway."

How's the head?"

She smiled when his hand ran over her hair as he passed her.

"Hi. Head's okay now, but it was nice of you to bring lunch."

He grinned. "I'm a nice guy, haven't you heard?"

"I don't know how I could have missed it." She smiled innocently. "Did you get the shots you needed?"

"Yes. All done. We can do whatever you want this afternoon."

Unbidden, a series of images of what they could do all afternoon flashed in Clara's mind. Dirty, sexy images. Maybe the previous night's alcohol had removed those inhibitions permanently.

"If you don't have any ideas, I have plenty," he added, winking.

She laughed, feeling something shift into place. It appeared they were on the same page for the first time since Bali. For the life of her, she couldn't figure out why it had taken her so long to catch up to him.

Pushing away the untouched takeaway boxes, she crawled across the bed to where he was seated. The intrigued look on his face made her nervous, but she did her best to ignore them. Although she had no idea what had really removed the roadblock in her head, she wasn't about to let such a trivial thing as nerves put it back in place.

"You wanna tell me about those ideas?" she asked, feeling the nerves fade away as his breath quickened. "Or would you rather show me?"

"Are you still drunk?" he blurted after staring at her for a moment.

Apparently, they weren't on the same page, after all. Clara sat back on her knees and wondered if she should let embarrassment or amusement win. The situation solved itself when laughter bubbled up in her throat. No wonder Duncan didn't know what to make of her behavior. After all, she didn't know herself.

Duncan looked at her, amused. "Clue me in anytime."

Sputtering with giggles, she shook her head. "I think it's best if I don't. I'm not drunk."

"Good." His smile widened as he leaned in. "Then I can kiss you with a clear conscience."

Both giggles and concerns about who was on which page, died inside of Clara as Duncan captured her more than willing lips with his own. Even as fire erupted deep within her and her breath quickened, she felt a deep peace. This was right. Duncan was right.

The air in the room came alive with electricity. Clara let herself fall into a world where she and Duncan were the only people who existed. His lips explored, his hands adored, his whole body made her feel alive like she'd only ever been once before—in Bali.

She burned from the inside out with need for him. He was every bit as hot for her when they found each other and fell into the rhythm as old as time. Clara could have sworn the earth moved, simply clicked into place the way it was supposed to... Or something else overly romantic and clichéd.

Duncan's staccato breaths were loud in her ears, pulses and hearts hammering away as she came undone. Even as the world around her expanded to more than just the bed, the weight of him over her meant she could pretend a little while longer. Right there, nothing else was important.

* * * *

Duncan was stuck on Clara's mind like a piece of gum under her shoe. She knew it was bordering on ridiculous, but she couldn't stop thinking about him. The drive back from New York had passed in a flash. She'd been so caught up with the man next to her, she hadn't been paying attention when Grace called and asked them both for dinner that same evening.

It meant that instead of naked pizza or whatever brilliant idea she and Duncan could come up with if they'd been alone, they were now seated across from each other at the Quinn dining table making small talk while eating roast pork. Clara had never known such torture existed.

"We've been contacted by some journalists," Carl told Clara during dinner. "Are you interested in telling your story? They'd like both sides. There's also a morning TV show that would like our visit. It might be inspirational for others who are in the same situation."

Clara tore her attention away from Duncan and the not-so-pure thoughts she'd been having about him. Telling her story to a journalist or even worse, on TV, was pretty much the last thing she wanted. She could barely make sense of things yet in her head, in her own language. Trying to be articulate with a stranger on TV in her second language sounded like a disaster in the making.

"I'm not sure…"

"It would be wonderful to help keep the hope alive for others," Grace said, smiling.

Clara sighed. How was she supposed to object to that? "Can I think about it?"

"Sure." Grace smiled again, but it was clear she was disappointed.

"Maybe you should write the book you've been talking about instead, Papa Q," Duncan commented while helping himself to another serving of pie.

A book sounded much better in Clara's opinion. You could take your time with a book and find the right words without the pressure of a microphone in your face. She didn't say anything, though. It was mostly the Quinns' story, after all. She'd showed up, but she hadn't been searching for and missing anyone for almost three decades.

"Maybe," Carl half-agreed and then changed the subject. "I talked to the principal at the high school the other day, Clara. He has an opening in the art department, if you're interested. I told him how talented you are."

Grace picked up where her husband left off before Clara could respond. "And there's an apartment available just down the street if you get tired of staying at Luke's. Of course, you're always welcome to move in here."

Fighting the urge to cry, Clara cleared her throat at the same time as Duncan. She couldn't look at him, knowing if she saw the look of understanding on his face that she expected, there was no way she could hold the tears back. "Thank you for thinking of me, but I can't. I have to go home soon."

"But your family is here," Grace pointed out. "You said yourself you have no family left in Denmark."

"I have a life there—friends, work connections, memories."

Grace stiffly sipped her wine. "You could have a life here if you wanted. With a family who loves you. Doesn't that mean anything to you?"

She didn't get it. Clara bit back all the ugly words that welled up inside her head. "Of course it does. But my roots are somewhere else.

Until you realize that, I can't start to put down new ones here."

"You're either a Quinn or you're not," Carl said. The silence that followed was deafening. Clara didn't know where the ultimatums were suddenly coming from. Her first impression of Carl had been positive, but it had been awhile since she'd spent any time with him. Did she even know him?

"That's just it. I'm not a Quinn. I don't know how to be one. I don't know how to be Eve Quinn and the person you're expecting me to be. Even if I did, I wouldn't be able to be her without turning my back on the person I've been for as long as I can remember. How can you ask that of someone?"

"You were born as Eve Quinn. It's who you are." Stubbornly, Carl kept eating as if he wasn't in the middle of an argument.

"I can't be anyone but Clara. Not for you, not for anyone." Standing up, she took a deep breath. "I don't want to fight with you. Thank you for dinner, but I think it's best if I leave. Goodnight."

No one stopped her, but as she walked out, she heard Duncan get up. "I'll stay out of it for now, but don't make me take sides. You might not like the side I take. Goodnight."

He caught up with her outside and grabbed her hand without saying anything. Clara felt her heart being ripped in two. He was developing the ability to know exactly what she needed. It hurt because she suddenly knew that what she'd said inside was true. She had to go home soon. She couldn't make up her mind about anything as long as Copenhagen felt more and more like a distant dream where everything had been easier and less complicated.

"Thank you," she whispered and stopped walking so she could see him in the dark. "I know I said I'd come home with you, but I need some time alone to think. Is that okay?"

"Of course," he replied and drew her in for a kiss. "Whatever you need, baby. I'm sorry they don't get it."

She drew in a shuddering breath and allowed herself to linger in his embrace for a moment. Why didn't things ever work out smoothly? "You know I have to go home, right?"

"I know. I hate it, but I know."

"Will we… Will we be okay?"

He pulled back and cupped her face in his hands. "You and I have been through worse. We will be more than okay."

Clara nodded, sure she would cry if she tried to talk. So maybe things didn't work out smoothly, but perhaps they did work out somehow.

Chapter Fifteen

Duncan had messed up the flooring he was attempting to finish in one of the upstairs bedrooms twice before he'd finally given up. The satisfaction he usually felt when working on the house was missing. Instead, he felt like finding the biggest hammer he had and just start bashing things. Of course, that would be neither satisfactory nor make the fact that Clara was leaving, less true.

He'd known all along she'd go back to Denmark at some point, but he'd refused to think about it. The only comfort was that he'd have her real phone number this time, but when he thought about it properly, he wasn't comforted at all. He'd gotten used to having her around. Seeing her whenever he wanted, kissing her, loving her and feeling her respond to even his smallest touch. Soon, she'd be halfway around the world. Asleep when he was awake and awake when he was asleep. Spending her days speaking a language he didn't understand and living in a city and a country he'd never visited. She'd have fun with friends he'd never met. Paint pictures of places he'd never seen.

It wasn't just jealousy bubbling up inside of him; it was also fear and frustration. Fear that he'd never get her back the way he wanted to and frustration that there was nothing he could do about it. In some ways, it was like his life had stopped abruptly. What was the point of going through the motions when everything he wanted was on another continent?

He hadn't asked her to stay. He'd wanted to, but it would have been too selfish. He'd seen it when Grace and Cark had assumed so naturally that her life was with them now. He couldn't belittle the life Clara had somewhere else. He couldn't hurt her that way.

It had been obvious how she'd struggled to fit in, not just with the family, but in a strange country. She had a life in Denmark. He'd also considered going with her, but he didn't know for certain that she'd want him to. Drunken ramblings didn't count, and he'd been too much of a coward to ask when she was sober.

He downed the beer and went into the kitchen to grab another one, his third since the failed flooring project. Or maybe fourth. Just as he was considering grabbing the fifth so he wouldn't have to get up from the couch in ten minutes, there was a knock on the door.

Clara was outside, looking like a something out of a fairytale. It had started snowing, and melting snow was glistening in her hair. For a moment, he just stared at her, almost afraid that she wasn't real.

"Hi."

The sound of her voice broke him out of his daze. "Hi. Come on in."

"Thanks."

He took her coat and shamelessly ogled her as she bent down to untie her boots. "Did you walk out here?"

"Yeah. It was beautiful in the snow." She smiled and ran her fingers through her damp hair. Her cheeks were red from the cold. He couldn't help himself any longer. He cupped her face and kissed her cold lips like a man who knew he'd be starving from the taste of her soon.

It was hard to step back, but he did it anyway. "But it's cold. And dark."

"It's not so bad. The snow lights everything up. Plus, it's not cold when you're moving." She tilted her head and studied him. "You don't have to worry about me, you know. I live in a big city. I can take care of myself."

He didn't doubt her, but he wanted to be the one to take care of her. She had to know that. "I know."

Trying to be stealthy, Duncan put the beer bottles away and got them something hot to drink. No matter what Clara said, it was cold out. He didn't want her to get sick.

A little while later, when they were seated next to each other on the couch with steaming mugs and a crackling fireplace across the room, he could barely remember the frustration he'd felt earlier. Clara was there and that was all he wanted to focus on. There would be plenty of time for frustration the following day once she'd left Stonebridge, Connecticut, America and the continent. The frustration bubbled up in his throat again.

"Damn." She sighed. "Walking out here, I had all this courage. Now, it's drowned in tea."

"Why do you need courage? And how did you manage to escape your farewell party?"

"You mean the farewell party you didn't attend? Easy. I told them I had a headache. Which wasn't even a lie until I got some fresh air." Putting the mug down, she turned to look at him. "I needed courage to come here. I wasn't sure you'd want to see me since you didn't come to say goodbye."

"I wasn't going to let you go without saying goodbye," he said softly, partly regretting that he hadn't showed up anyway. He knew Mama and Papa Q hadn't been there either. "I was just in a bad mood tonight and didn't want to ruin anything. I hate that you're leaving."

"Me too. Sometimes, at least. Other times I miss my life in Denmark. My friends, my home, my things."

He nodded, unable to blame her. He knew what traveling was like. However, he'd never been gone as long as she had. There always came a certain point when you were just ready for your own bed. It was just too bad he'd rather have her in his bed than have her go home to her own.

"I hate how I'm leaving things, though. With Grace and Carl." She sighed. "It's been so tense, almost impossible, since dinner last week. Every time I try to talk to them, they dig their heels in. They don't, or won't, understand why I can't be someone who has existed in their minds for so many years. You know, at first they'd ask about my life back home, but lately they just ignore it. In their minds, I magically went from being five months old to being all grown up. It's ridiculous."

"I know. I wish I could tell you what their problem is, but I don't get it either. None of us does. I'm so sorry they're not showing you what wonderful people they can be. It's such a waste after spending so much time wishing to get you back."

Clara smiled sadly. "There's nothing more I can do. What's more important is that I also hate how I'm leaving things with you."

"At least it's better than last time."

She laughed humorlessly. "Yeah…"

Reaching for her hand, he tugged her until she was facing him.

"Look, as much as I hate that you're leaving, I understand why you have to. I'm not Grace or Carl. I get it, Clara."

"I know." She let out a shuddering breath. "That just makes it harder. If you'd been angry, then we could slam the doors and just... God, this sucks. I'm sorry, Duncan. I know I'm being a selfish bitch, pulling you in different directions. First, I push you away, then I pull you close and then I push you away again."

"My own personal Clara roller coaster." He did his best to smile. "Just promise me that I'll see you again."

"You'll see me again." The words came fast like bullets. "I'm not turning my back on any of you, but I can't turn my back on my past either. I have to figure out where I fit in... To combine the Christensen part of me with the Quinn part. I can't do that right now with Grace and Carl pushing me."

"Don't give up on me yet," she begged.

He pulled her into his arms and buried his face in her hair. "I couldn't."

Duncan wished he could tell her that he knew exactly where she fit in. With *him*. That wasn't the answer she was looking for. Even if she accepted it as the truth eventually, she had to find the answer herself. Pushing her like Grace and Carl was not an option. He'd only end up pushing her away completely.

That night their lovemaking was hurried and desperate. Intense to the point of madness. Duncan tried to evict all thoughts of the next day from his head, but it was almost impossible. Not even the damp skin, sinful curves and breathy sighs of the woman surrounding him could make him forget she'd be gone soon.

He held her as close as he dared until morning came in all its relentless glory. He hadn't slept. Although they hadn't talked, he had a feeling Clara hadn't either.

So many times a plea had been on his lips, but he knew he couldn't ask her to stay any more than he could offer to go with her. It had come to him just before dawn. The Quinns had spent decades trying to find Eve. He had tried to find Clara for two years. They had all found what they were looking for. The time had come for Clara to find what *she* was looking for. Duncan only hoped she'd discover that he fit into her life somehow. If not, then he was up to the challenge of convincing her. Until then, he'd have to take the pain like a man. At least she'd promised to visit. They'd talked about him visiting, too.

The 'taking the pain like a man' part sounded good in theory, at least. But when he saw her tear-filled eyes and her zombie-like wave at the airport, he wished he was young enough to go cry into his mommy's skirt.

Since that was out of the question, he turned to Luke, the only one besides himself who had been allowed to take Clara to the airport. "I need a drink."

"Me, too," Luke agreed. "But I have to open the shop in a couple of hours and it's barely eight in the morning. Maybe coffee would be better?"

"Fuck coffee." Duncan stalked off, deciding that he couldn't be expected to be polite at least for a few days.

"Dude." Luke caught up with him outside. "You're not the only one who thinks it blows majorly that she's leaving. But we knew she would have to go home eventually."

"I know." He looked around for something to punch, but the only thing available was Luke.

"You love her, don't you?" Luke asked as they reached the car.

Duncan snorted. "What gave it away?"

Luke emitted an exasperated sigh. "You're not going to go buy another rundown house to fix up, are you?"

"No. No more houses. I'm going to go with alcohol this time."

"Yeah, that sounds a lot healthier. I'm glad we had this little chat." Luke rolled his eyes. "How long are you going to be a drama queen?"

"I'm not being a drama queen." Duncan got into the car. "And as long as I fucking want to."

"If you wait to hit the booze until I get off work tonight, I'm buying the first round."

Duncan considered the offer on the drive back to Stonebridge. He considered it as he tried to focus on work. But by mid-afternoon, he decided to reject it, so he found the nearest bar and ordered the first of many whiskeys.

There were no truths at the bottom of the glass, and the alcohol didn't make the constant pain in his chest go away. Instead, it just made him tired and incapable of thinking straight. Not thinking straight meant that he steadily forgot all the reasons he hadn't stopped or gone with Clara. That in turn, made his mood even worse.

 He was complaining about how much life sucked to the bartender when there was a tap on his shoulder.

"Dude, when are you going to stop whining and move away from the bar? We're trying to order here."

Duncan was pretty sure he'd seen the very agitated guy before, but since his memory was marinating in whiskey, he had no idea where. "Go away," he told him.

"You go away," said the angry guy, pushing his way to the bar at Duncan's expense. "It's not like you need any more to drink anyway."

Trying not to topple over on his stool, Duncan was vaguely aware that there was a choice in front of him—a choice that included a good decision and a bad decision. But that was as far as he could think. So he pushed back.

A second later, he was on the floor, learning the hard way, just what kind of decision he'd made. Could you actually hear your ribs breaking or did whiskey sloshing around inside of you make the same sound? Duncan groaned and tried to get up. Or away from the kicking. When angry dude was yanked away by someone, he wanted to kiss that someone out of relief.

It turned out to be Luke, the knight in shining jeans. Duncan chuckled and winced as Luke helped him stand up.

"Seriously?" Luke sighed. "You're a danger to yourself, man."

"Yeah," Duncan agreed easily. "I need a drink."

"Not happening. Let me pay your tab, and then we're out of here."

"No."

Luke sighed. "Don't be a spoiled brat. It only works for Rachel."

"Rachel is a girl." Duncan chuckled. At least Luke couldn't argue against that.

"Jesus Christ. Why me?" Luke left him, and Duncan focused his energy to stay upright. Some stuff was underrated. Or overrated. He couldn't remember the difference.

* * * *

It was painfully light in the room when he woke up. Bleary-eyed, he reached for his phone to check what time it was, but it wasn't on the nightstand as he'd expected. His head throbbed mercilessly. He reluctantly dragged himself out of bed to go to the bathroom. It wasn't until then that he realized he wasn't in his own house. He was in Luke's. More precisely, he was in the bathroom that until the previous day had been Clara's. Why didn't Luke just shoot him and be done with it?

He didn't remember leaving the bar the previous night, but he remembered being more wasted than he'd been in years. More wasted than Clara had been in New York. He sighed. Everything came back to Clara.

"Morning," Luke greeted him when Duncan eventually entered the kitchen.

Duncan grunted and headed straight for the coffeepot.

"You left your cell phone in the hallway last night. I've been taking calls all morning because the damn thing kept ringing. Emily is pissed because you didn't show up for work today. It's funny how she sounds like she's your boss and not the other way around, huh?" Luke pointed to the counter. "Hangover breakfast. All fried. You're welcome."

Sitting down and blowing on the scalding coffee so he could inhale it the way he wanted to, Duncan gave a nod of appreciation. "Thanks. 'Brother of the Year Award' is yours."

"Thought so. Mom also called. And Rachel. There are texts from Clara, but I didn't read them. She sent me one, too. She arrived home safely and plans to sleep for about a week."

Duncan reached out for his phone. "That's good to hear. I'll call Mama Q and Rachel later. And I'll go to the studio in a while and deal with Emily. She just likes to nag."

"I think she was worried," Luke commented.

"Yeah..." Duncan stopped paying attention and opened the first of Clara's four new texts. He should have texted her yesterday. Even though she would have been in the air, she could have gotten them as soon as she'd turned her phone on. He sucked.

The first one simply read 'I miss you,' and he almost let the phone drop to the floor when he saw when it had been sent—just a few minutes after they'd said goodbye at the airport. Just when he thought he couldn't feel any worse. If he'd seen the text when he'd received it, he'd probably be in Denmark now.

The second one was during her short layover in Frankfurt. She wrote that she wanted to fly back to America instead of continuing on to Denmark. The next one was from Copenhagen right after she'd landed, and the final one was sent when she'd arrived at her apartment. It read that she was going to bed and she missed him.

He quickly texted back even though he knew she'd probably be sleeping. He needed to find out the exact time difference. And maybe take more assignments so he could pay what he suspected might become an enormous phone bill. The whole drinking thing couldn't happen again. Not just because hangovers only got worse with age and his ribs hurt like hell, but also because it wasn't who he was. He was constructive, not destructive.

"Thanks for putting up with me yesterday." He looked at Luke, who was twirling his own cell phone around on the table.

"It's not right." Luke pushed away his phone so it almost knocked over his coffee mug. "I resent Mom and Dad for pushing her away. We'd only just gotten her back. You know what I mean. They only had to open their eyes and see her. *Really* see her. Not Eve. Not a baby. But Clara. *Our* Clara."

Suddenly very sober, Duncan rubbed his forehead. "I agree that they played a role in her leaving when and how she did, but she would have gone back anyway. If not now, then later. I think she had to in order to figure stuff out. Her life was turned upside down, man. She was rattled. You saw that. Trust me, the woman I met in Bali was not rattled."

Luke seemed to be in his own world. Duncan doubted he was even listening. "You know what I regret? Never visiting Danny and Linda in Copenhagen. I would have felt Clara as clearly as I did that first day when she came here. I would have known." Luke nodded to himself.

"At least we know where she is now, right?"

Luke looked up. His expression said it all. It wasn't as big a comfort as it should have been.

Chapter Sixteen

Setting foot on Danish soil again felt almost surreal. Clara felt like she had been gone for years. Everything was as she'd left it, but she was a completely different woman than when she left. She'd left as one hundred percent Clara Christensen, but she returned with a great deal of Eve Quinn mixed into her soul. She wasn't sure if she was embracing that part of her or trying to reject it.

"You're here! Welcome home!" Marie came running full speed and hugged Clara the moment she stepped through the doors to the unrestricted part of the arrival area.

"Hi!" Clara soaked up the hug, grateful that her friend had made the trip across the country to welcome her home. "It's so good to see you again."

"Right back at you, American girl." Marie grinned and grabbed hold of the luggage cart, steering them through the masses of people. "So, tell me everything."

Clara laughed weakly. "Do you have a couple of weeks?"

"Well, no. I have until tonight. I could only get today off work. But it's a four-hour drive home."

"I appreciate you going all this way just for a few hours. I've really missed you."

She wasn't in the mood for going out to dinner with Marie, but with her friend living at the opposite end of the country, she didn't know when she'd see her again. So she gave in, trying to ignore the invisible travel grime she would have loved to wash off before doing anything else.

Duncan was on her mind as she tried to keep up with Marie's chatter and the sound of Danish voices all around her again.

"You're not listening," Marie informed her while she was poking at her steak, sitting at the local steak house not far from Clara's apartment.

Clara smiled apologetically. "I'm sorry. I think the traveling is catching up with me, plus it's so weird to hear Danish all the time again."

"Understandable. So, what are you going to do now? I mean, you quit the high school and all."

Shrugging, Clara reached for her wine glass. "I don't know. To be honest, I don't know much of anything right now. I guess I need to figure it out."

"You will. I know this whole thing threw you for a loop, but you'll dig out the old, levelheaded Clara again."

"I hope so. I really do."

A neighbor had looked after Clara's apartment while she was gone, so she didn't come home to a thick layer of dust and dead orchids in the windows. But the place felt off somehow. She didn't bother unpacking, just took a quick shower before collapsing into bed. Her own bed. Nothing felt off about that. It was like heaven.

* * * *

She woke late the next morning. At first, she didn't remember where she was, but then she recognized the sounds of the busy street outside and sighed. She was home. Dragging herself out of bed and into the kitchen, she realized she needed a trip to the grocery store down on the corner before she could have even a cup of coffee.

The quick trip for groceries soon became a walk through the familiar streets instead. She stopped for a cup of coffee and then walked around the lakes she loved so much, breathing in the city. Exhaust fumes to some, but home to Clara.

After her small-town American adventure, she appreciated her beloved city even more. The hustle and bustle, the convenience of everything being in one place and the history that poured out of the crevices in the old buildings. She almost felt a part of that history. She reached the citadel, which was one of her favorite places in the world and joined the people running and walking around the star-shaped piece of land. As always, it made her thankful to live in such a beautiful city.

It was still too early to call anyone in Stonebridge, so Clara had time to reflect on some of the things that had happened since she last walked there. She was so deep in thought that it took her a few moments to realize her cell phone was ringing. Duncan was up early.

"I nearly called Gertrud for old times' sake," he greeted her when she picked up.

Clara laughed. "I'm sure she'd appreciate your call. Maybe I should go visit her."

"She'd love that." Just the sound of his voice thousands of miles away made her smile. It also made her want to jump on a plane to go back to him.

"So, what's it like being home again?" he asked.

Looking around, Clara sighed. "Good. Surreal. Weird. Lonely. Take your pick."

"What's *your* pick?"

"Surreal," she admitted, glancing at the grey skies and deciding to find shelter before it started raining. "As surreal as when I first came to Stonebridge. It kind of freaks me out that when I look at my life, it's like it belongs to someone else. I don't recognize it."

"Give it time, baby. I'm sure it will all become clear to you soon. And when it does…" He cleared his throat. "So, are you going to look for another job or what?"

Wondering why he'd changed the subject so swiftly, she realized she didn't know the answer to his question. "Probably." She needed to make a living, but she didn't know where and how she wanted to make that living.

When they'd ended the conversation, Clara sighed. How easy it would be to run back to him and pretend it was the only thing that mattered? He cared, it was so obvious. And her love for him ran deeper than anything she'd ever felt. It should be so easy. But it was because of how much she loved him that he deserved the best of her. The best of her was not a rag doll being pulled in different directions. She couldn't go to him unless she found the inner calm she'd once possessed.

The afternoon and evening stretched out endlessly in front of her. She wasn't in the mood to see anyone even though she had been gone for a long time. The people she wanted to be with were halfway across the world.

She started to go through the big pile of mail and found a letter from the principal of the school where she had worked. He was offering her old job back whenever she was ready, telling her the students and her old colleagues missed her. That was one problem solved, only Clara wasn't positive she liked the solution.

Throwing the letter on the table, she picked up her phone. She would need a job soon to pay off the phone bill. Or at least coordinate her calls so they could use Skype. Texting Duncan first, she then stared at the number for the Quinn house for a few minutes before sighing and calling Luke. Even though she knew exactly where her twin brother was, she agreed with him that the whole being separated thing sucked. How had she ever lived without these people?

"Hey, sis. I was just about to call you."

"Apparently you're too slow."

He laughed. "It would seem so. How's it going?"

Plopping down on the couch, she sighed. "It's not. I'm not sure going home was the right decision. I miss you guys."

"No more than we miss you, be certain of that."

"I feel horrible about the way I left. Did Grace and Carl say anything?"

"I haven't talked to them yet," Luke admitted. "They crossed the line, Clara. We all agree and we're behind you. At first, I thought they just needed time to realize that their baby Eve grew into a grown woman named Clara, but now I don't know. All these years... All we wanted was to get you back. Then we did. They have no right to ruin it."

"I ruined your family."

"No, you didn't. You completed it."

Clara sighed. "I used to think the worst part was ringing that doorbell that first day and introducing myself, but that turned out to be the easy part."

"I think that's the root of the problem. Expectations. You shouldn't think that Mom and Dad are disappointed in you in any way. I just think their expectations weren't realistic. Their version of Eve, the one who's lived in their heads and hearts all those years, she'd be theirs, you know? Logically, they knew that if you were alive, someone else would have raised you. But the alternate version of you lived in their hearts for so long. And you weren't it."

"It's possible. I wouldn't blame them for that. I know that if I'd had more time, I would have conjured up my own ideas about what my birth parents should or would be like." She twisted a lock of hair around her finger. "I just don't know what to do."

"There's nothing you can do. There's nothing any of us can do. Talking to them hasn't helped, so they have to open their eyes all on their own."

"If that lawyer hadn't killed himse—"

"Don't say that," Luke interrupted harshly before continuing more softly. "Don't even think it. Forget about Mom and Dad for a moment and think about how happy you've made the rest of the family. And hopefully, also yourself."

The smile unfolded naturally on her face. "I will never be able to find the words to describe how happy I am that I discovered the truth and found you guys. I've known you my whole life, Luke. I just didn't know it. That's what it feels like."

"Very fitting." The smile was evident in his voice and proved Clara's point. Her own smile grew, no other words needed to be spoken.

* * * *

Unable to sleep the following morning, Cara got up early and headed out into the darkness for an early morning run. Her mom, her *adoptive* mom, had always hated her running in the dark, but Clara knew to stick to the well-lit streets where there were people out, no matter how late or early it was.

It was Thanksgiving. Not a holiday she'd ever celebrated or given much thought, but knowing her family would be together on this day, made her long for Connecticut even more than usual.

In Denmark, it was just a regular Thursday. With no other plans for the day, she traveled forty minutes north of the city on the train to where she'd grown up. The cemetery was within easy walking distance from the train station. The last time she'd been there was the day before she left for America when she'd apologized to a slab of stone bearing her adoptive parents' names and hoped they'd understand what she was doing.

Now, she knew they did. Even though she'd never been a fan of organized religion, she couldn't help but believe that there was something after death. It didn't need a name to be real. She was perfectly content to close her eyes and talk through her heart to the two people who had raised her and loved her as much as any parents anywhere could have.

As she stood looking at the tombstone, she admitted to herself that the little plot of grass that their urns rested beneath was one of the biggest ties she had to Denmark. She couldn't just pick up the phone or Skype with a tombstone. As if Birthe and Erik Christensen lived in a hole in the ground...

"I'm sorry, Mom and Dad," Clara whispered, wishing it wasn't too cold and wet to sit on the grass. "I'm being stupid, aren't I? You're in my heart. Not in the ground. And you wouldn't want anything but my happiness. Just... Give a girl a hint, would you?"

No hint appeared. She shook her head at herself. Maybe the answer was therapy since she was apparently going crazy.

Walking back to the station, she passed a local gallery owned by an old friend of her mother's. Clara had been coming there all her life, always fascinated with the art on the walls. The owner had taken an interest in Clara's work early on. She had a standing invitation to bring in whatever she wanted to sell. Clara just hated selling her work. It wasn't logical, but she'd never created to show off. She'd created because she couldn't help herself.

Before she could rethink her spontaneous decision, she walked into the gallery. Twenty minutes later, she had arranged to meet the gallery owner the following day at the storage space where she kept her art. It was time to stop being sentimental and liquidate.

That night, Clara turned on some music and sat down with a sketchpad, a glass of wine and the intention of not getting up before she knew who she was. She had two birth certificates in her possession, one for Eve and one for Clara, but they were no help. She had to look elsewhere.

For a long time, she just sat with her eyes closed and focused on the music. Then she reopened her eyes and attempted an exercise an old university professor had once told her about. Mind cleared of everything except one word, she drew instinctively and almost without registering it. It was time to find out where her subconscious self believed home was.

Clara struggled to keep her focus. After a few minutes, it was shattered completely when the phone rang. Reluctantly, she stood up to retrieve it from the coffee table. It was Rachel.

"Hey," Clara said.

There were only faint voices on the other end of the line. No exuberant sister.

"Hello? Rachel, can you hear me?"

Instead of Rachel, she heard Luke. His voice wasn't clear, so he probably wasn't talking into the phone. Clara frowned. Had Rachel called her by accident?

"It's my turn to give thanks this year," Clara heard Luke say. "Can I just say that I can never hope to make it as epic as Danny did last year." Laughter resonated in her ear. She smiled even though it was yet another Quinn thing about which she was clueless.

"One word says it all this year. Clara. I'm thankful for Clara. That she came back into our lives and she turned out to be nothing short of amazing. I just wish she was here." A choir of voices agreed, and Clara swallowed with some difficulty. What was she doing cooped up alone in her apartment in Copenhagen?

Others started talking, and she couldn't make out what was being said anymore. Just as she was about to hang up, she heard Rachel whisper, "I love you, sis." Then the call ended.

Almost on their own, her fingers typed a message to her sister, telling her thanks and that she loved her, too. Then she threw the phone on the couch and shook her head. If it wouldn't hurt so much, banging her head against the wall would be been her next move.

She had been such an idiot. *Family.* After being alone for two years, she had family. Yet, she was alone while they were celebrating a holiday together. It was her own fault. Grace and Carl might have pushed and pulled until she had come close to breaking in two, but they were right. Family was what mattered.

Powering up her laptop, Clara sat down and picked up the sketch she'd been working on when the phone had rang. Even incomplete, the resemblance was unmistakable. The teasing smile and the strong jaw.

Her home was not in Copenhagen or Stonebridge. It was with Duncan, wherever he was.

Chapter Seventeen

The day after Thanksgiving, Duncan was holed up in his office doing paperwork. Peter and Emily had the day off, but Duncan knew he had to keep busy to avoid sulking over Clara being halfway across the world. However, between handling the paperwork, he was checking for assignments. Overseas assignments. Preferably in Scandinavia. There weren't any, though. Closest one was in Portugal and that wasn't really close at all.

He sighed and wished he'd had a full day of appointments to distract himself. Who needed holidays anyway?

Thanksgiving had been... Duncan tapped a pen against the computer keyboard while he wrecked his brain trying to think of the right description for the recent holiday. After a few moments, he had it. *Ironic.* That was what it had been. Extremely ironic and extremely tense. Almost like a silent war.

Every single holiday he'd celebrated with the Quinns had been without Clara. Or Eve. She'd only been present by the white rose Luke had placed on the extra place setting every time. Despite her absence, the past holidays had been happy and filled with joy and laughter. He had a million good memories from each and every one of them.

Ironically enough, the first one since her reappearance in their lives had been the direct opposite. It wasn't even because she hadn't been there, though that was bad enough. It was because everyone knew one of the bigger reasons for her absence—Grace and Carl's merciless pressure on her and inability to accept her without reservations.

Luke had silently protested by bringing a rose like always. Rachel had rebelled by asking a few days in advance, if they could substitute the traditional turkey with duck. Grace had agreed easily enough. It wasn't until Danny asked why at the table that Rachel had smiled brightly and revealed her rebellion. She took great pleasure in sharing the details about a semi-holiday in late November where Danes ate roast duck.

Each year for Thanksgiving, one member of the family would say a few words about what they were grateful for. Luke's turn had been up, and his focus had been on Clara for obvious reasons. The conversation had centered on her, too. Both Mama and Papa Q had been unusually quiet. Even though he hated the strain in the family, Duncan hoped it meant their consciences were catching up with their actions and words.

Duncan pushed away the paperwork. He wanted to call Clara, but she'd texted earlier and told him she'd be busy and that she would call him when she could. He tried to ignore the little jealous voice inside of him that was really curious about what she was busy with. She hadn't said.

Since calling Clara was out, he called Gertrud. He hadn't talked to her in a while, and he'd come to enjoy catching up with her every now and then.

"Duncan! I was just thinking about you and wondering how you were doing."

He smiled. He'd wished many times that he'd been lucky enough to have a grandmother like Gertrud. "We must be soul mates then, thinking about each other at the same time and all. Hello, Gertrud. How are you?"

"Oh, not much excitement goes on in an old woman's life," she replied. "Don't tell me you've misplaced your girl's number already."

Duncan laughed. For the first time, he noticed the hint of an Australian accent in Gertrud's words, no doubt a legacy from her late husband, mixed with the Danish accent he'd grown used to with Clara. "Oh no, I've got her number memorized. That doesn't mean I can't check in on you, though."

"I appreciate each and every call, you know that. Especially now that you know who you're calling." She chuckled. "So, how are you really doing?"

Hesitating, Duncan pushed a pen around on the desk in front of him. "Clara went home. I think the best thing I can do for her is give her a little space and time, but I'm not sure."

"Some people say I'm crazy and maybe they're right, but I've always believed in fate. What's meant to be will be. Look at me. I had to find a man worthy of my heart on the other side of the globe. I think every girl needs some time and space once in a while. Just not too much."

"Got it. I appreciate the advice."

"What else are old people good for?"

"That's harsh and very untrue," he objected.

"Maybe a little untrue," she admitted with a laugh. "But not completely. My arthritis is flaring up, so I'm a little cranky. I was almost finished with a pair of socks for my neighbor's son. Such bad timing."

"He'll have to freeze."

Gertrud laughed again. "You're better than a mood pill, Duncan Cantwell."

They chatted for a while longer and when the call ended, Duncan had to admit that Gertrud was quite the mood pill herself.

Out of patience, he called Clara, but the line was busy. Then he called Luke, only to hear laughing and Luke's ringtone outside the office door.

"You rang?" Luke said, entering the office. "You should really lock the door. Anyone could just walk in."

"They just did," Duncan replied dryly. "What are you doing here?"

"Just wanted to see where you were placed on the sulking scale today, that's all. Why were you calling me?"

"Sulking scale," Duncan muttered. "I'm not sulking."

"Of course not." Chuckling, Luke threw himself in a chair. "So?"

Duncan turned in his own chair. "Do you think civil war would break out if I, or *we*, which was what I wanted to talk to you about, weren't here for Christmas?"

Luke smiled knowingly. "Ah, yes. I hear Denmark's lovely this time of year. Snow and ice and blistering cold rain."

"Exactly."

"Well, if that's where we want to go, then that's where we'll go. We're big boys. We don't have to ask permission. Rachel will want to come, too."

"And Mama and Papa Q?" Duncan asked. Even though they were the major reason Clara had left, they had still saved his life when he was a kid.

Finding Clara

"They'll have to deal." Luke shrugged. "It's not an unknown kidnapper keeping us all apart anymore. It's them."

Duncan mulled it over. Things were changing and it could be for the best if only... He sighed. Eve Quinn was no longer missing. He'd found Clara Christensen again. And he was still stuck on *if only*.

"Dude, you're sulking," Luke interrupted his thoughts. "Let's go raid Ben's fridge for lunch. Vanessa is out shopping with Linda and Rachel."

The mention of Vanessa's cooking cheered Duncan up momentarily. He turned off his computer. "Dibs on the pie."

But because it was just that kind of day, Danny had already eaten all the pie when Luke and Duncan arrived at Ben's.

"Dude. Weren't you taught to share?"

Danny cackled. "Not the good stuff."

"Ass," Duncan muttered. "Are there any cookies?"

"He got to those, too. He's a bottomless pit. And it's my damn house!" Ben shook his head and handed a fussy Leanne over to Duncan.

"Hey, sweetheart. Of course you want your Uncle Dunc instead of Daddy. You've got great taste, don't you?"

"She needs a nap," Ben told him.

"And I look like a bed?"

"Kinda, yeah."

"Daddy's crazy," Duncan told Leanne, who smiled sleepily. "All right, naptime for pretty little girls."

He took her to her room and didn't even have time to sing her a song or read a story before she was asleep. He wished all girls were as uncomplicated as Leanne Quinn. She'd never encountered a problem that her Uncle Duncan couldn't handle.

"So, Duncan and I are going to Denmark for Christmas," Luke was saying as Duncan reentered the living room. The Quinn brothers were sprawled out on various pieces of furniture eating leftovers and drinking beer. Classy bunch. Duncan chuckled and snapped a picture with his cell phone.

"I'm in," Danny said immediately. "Where else would we go for Christmas? Danes eat this thing all December, like pancake balls, they're awesome. I bet Clara knows how to make them. You need a special pan and all."

"Seriously." Luke sighed. "Could you get your mind off food for just a moment?"

"I think everyone's in," Ben said, acting as the voice of reason as he'd done so many times over the years when conversations or discussions ran wild. "Vanessa and I have been talking about going to see Clara next year anyway. Assuming she didn't come back, of course. We made the mistake of mentioning Legoland to Tommy…"

"Uncle Danny's favorite little guy," Danny stated.

"Awesome. Go to Legoland and eat pancake balls? I'm going there for Clara." Duncan huffed and sat down while checking his phone. Why didn't she call? And who the hell went to Denmark because of pancake balls? What *were* pancake balls anyway?

"Don't be a girl," Danny replied. "We're all going there to see Clara, but that doesn't mean we can't do other things. None of you ever came to see Linda and me while we were there. I can show you lots of stuff. I've still got buddies there. It will be good to go back."

"Who's going to tell Mom and Dad?"

Duncan looked over at Ben, who genuinely looked afraid to tell his parents that he was going away for the holidays and tried not to laugh. Danny and Luke weren't as successful.

"You're killing me, bro," Danny said, chuckling. "We'll draw straws, okay? Will that make you feel better?"

Jumping up from the couch when his cell phone rang and escaping into the kitchen, Duncan never heard Ben's reply.

"Finally," he said in lieu of a greeting before even realizing it.

Clara's pretty laugh washed over him. "I'm sorry. I had a lot of stuff to take care of. Missing me?"

"Oh, maybe a tiny bit. When I'm bored."

"I love you, too."

Duncan sucked in a breath. Was she serious?

"I mean, I…" she started to amend before sighing. "Okay. No points for execution, obviously. Distance, over the phone… Yeah, sucks. But I do."

The smile was threatening to break his face in two. "Do what?"

"You're an ass," she complained. "Are you really going to make me say it again?"

"Say what again?"

"Okay, I changed my mind. Nothing." He could hear her trying to suppress her laughter.

Luke came into the kitchen. "Is that Clara?"

Duncan scowled. "Yes, it's Clara and you're interrupting a pretty important conversation, so buzz off."

"Hey, Clara!" Luke yelled, earning himself a look that could kill from Duncan.

"Tell Luke I'll call him later and tell him my news," Clara said.

"What news?" Duncan asked.

"She's got news?" Luke butted in.

Duncan rolled his eyes and started pushing Luke out of the kitchen. "Hey, Danny. A hand here, please?"

"Hey! Who died and made you king of Ben's kitchen?" Luke complained.

Clara was laughing into Duncan's ear as he struggled to hold onto the phone and push Luke out at the same time. "You guys are so funny."

Finally, Danny came and took care of Luke, making it possible for Duncan to close the door and sigh with relief. It only took a few seconds for Ben to start yelling at them not to break the furniture.

"Okay, where were we?" Duncan asked Clara.

"In opposite corners of the world," she replied softly. "I was being classy by telling you that I love you for the first time over the damn phone."

"Allow me to sink to your level, then. I love you, too, Clara. You have no idea." The elation couldn't quite mask the pain of being so far away from her, but almost.

She laughed softly. "Oh, I see how it is. I'm dragging you down. Too bad we're so far apart right now. I bet I could drag you down even further if we were together."

He closed his eyes and imagined some of the ways she could drag him down. Crap. Why the hell was he in Ben's kitchen instead of in his own house? "I bet you could, baby."

"Shit," she swore suddenly. "There's someone else calling me. I have to take it, it's about my art. Can we talk later?"

"Of course. Go deal with what you have to."

"All right. I love you. Bye."

Chuckling as he declared his love to the dial tone, he remembered that she hadn't shared her news. Then he shook his head. He had heard all the news he needed. Clara loved him. Nothing could tear him down now.

"Mom called," Luke told him when he came back into the living room. "She wants us all to come over for dinner again tonight. To talk."

"Screw that," Danny said and turned on the TV. "They should be talking to Clara, not us."

"At the moment, Mom and Dad are causing the problems in the family, but if we start acting like spoiled kids, too, then we're just as bad," Ben lectured.

Danny gave him an unimpressed glare. "Shut up. No one asked you to make sense."

"He's right." Duncan sighed. The woman he loved—that brought a smile to his face—had just found a family she didn't know existed. The least he could do for her was keep it together long enough for her to actually enjoy it. "We can at least hear what they've got to say."

"All right, all right." Danny held up his hands. "Geez."

* * * *

The mood at the Quinn House had not thawed out any since the previous day. Duncan couldn't remember ever feeling so awkward in the house he'd loved more than any other before.

"Hey, what was Clara's news?" Luke whispered from next to him on the couch. No one had ever whispered in the Quinn house before. It was ridiculous.

"Someone called about her art, so she never had a chance to tell me," Duncan replied.

"Maybe she got a new job," Luke suggested.

"Maybe." Duncan didn't like that idea much even though he knew she had to make a living. Anything that would make her stay in Denmark permanently wasn't good. Or maybe it didn't matter. People wanted pictures taken everywhere, so he could set up shop in Copenhagen. He'd need to give that some thought.

"Thank you for coming tonight," Papa Q said as he came in and sat down in his chair by the fireplace. It had always been his and when he'd first joined the family, Duncan had found security in it long before he'd found it in the man himself. Mama Q stood beside him, never one to sit down while dinner was cooking. She was wringing her hands in her apron, looking visibly distraught. Duncan hated to see her that way, but he'd picked Clara's side before even realizing it.

"What's up, Pop?" Danny asked. He never called his dad *Pop*. It sounded almost mockingly.

"Grace and I are going to Denmark," Papa Q announced.

"Great. The more, the merrier." Danny shook his head with a smile that wasn't the least bit amused.

"What do you mean?" Mama Q asked.

"It means we're all going to Denmark for Christmas," Luke replied. "Clara going home... It's killing me. Tearing me up inside now that I know what it's like to have her around all the time. It turned out, I wasn't the only one missing her already. So we're going."

"If this is the confession part of the evening, then I might as well tell you that I intend to stay if she's not coming back here," Duncan said. They probably all knew just by looking at him, but there had been enough miscommunications in the family lately. "If asking doesn't work, I'll be moving on to persuasion and begging."

"Woohoo!" Danny cheered and got up to slap Duncan on the back. "Get your girl, man. Get her to come home!"

Duncan smiled. "That's not a deal breaker. I can take pictures anywhere."

He turned his head when Mama Q's breath caught and she turned to leave. Sighing, he stood up to follow her, wondering what her reaction meant. She and Papa Q had made their bed, but they refused to lie in it apparently.

Chapter Eighteen

Clara had a very productive Friday. The art dealer had purchased all but one painting from her storage room. Clara was proud of herself for only hanging onto one piece. It was a portrait of her now long-gone invisible friend, Balder, that she planned to give to Luke. The likeliness between them was *not* invisible.

"I need to ask you a huge favor," she told Marie when she called her after lunch.

"Hello to you, too, sunshine. What's up?"

"I updated my ESTA, booked a plane ticket and I'll start packing this afternoon."

Marie giggled. "About time you figured it out, sweetie. Need me to sell the apartment?"

"No." Clara smiled at the thought of Marie knowing what was right all along but letting her figure it out for herself. "Christina next door is going to look after it. I'll be in contact with the real estate agent via phone."

"So what's the favor? A ride to the airport?"

"No, I need for you not to hate me."

"What?" Marie sounded amused.

"Well, I hated you a tiny bit when you moved across the country," Clara admitted, laughing softly. "So it would only be natural if you hated me for moving across the world."

"Are you kidding me? I do hate you. We'll never see each other. But I'm also happy for you. You're doing the right thing. Your family is over there. Duncan is over there. Your heart is over there. You have to go, I get that. I just want you to be happy."

"I am. I mean, I'm happy with my decision. I think I'll be happy over there. Before… Well, it was never meant as anything but a visit. It will be different this time."

"Are you trying to convince me or yourself?" Marie asked softly.

"Shut up." There was no malice in Clara's words, and she knew Marie wouldn't take offense. She would understand exactly what Clara meant because that was what best friends did.

However, it still nagged her later when she had started sorting through her things and packing what she couldn't possibly live without. Sometimes she was so sure about her decision, while other times she doubted she even knew what she was doing.

Her phone chimed, signaling a new e-mail. Clara seized the opportunity to take a break. Not just from the packing, but from her thoughts. It was a Facebook notification, telling her that one Rachel Quinn was requesting her friendship. It made Clara smile. She had her friendship already, but if Rachel needed it online too, Clara wasn't going to deny it to her. Even if she rarely ever visited the site. She couldn't even remember her own profile picture.

It was a much neglected profile that met Clara when she logged in. It hadn't been updated in forever. She supposed she should at least change the info about her work. After approving Rachel's request, she went to look at her sister's profile instead. Now there was a profile that didn't suffer from neglect. Apparently, Rachel was popular with more than four hundred friends. Clara doubted she'd even shook hands with that many people in her entire life.

She took some time to look at Rachel's photos. Through the tags, she found the profiles of her other siblings. There were a lot of funny pictures of them all together, some old, some new, even a few recent ones that she was in. One of them almost made her tear up. It looked so right. That was why she had made the right decision. She belonged somewhere.

Before signing off, she looked at her feed, updates made by people she had called friends, but who only lived in the suburbs of her life. One had gotten married; another was expecting her first child. A couple she knew was fighting and airing their dirty laundry right in her feed for everyone to see. All these people were living their lives with all their ups and downs, and Clara didn't know about any of it. In contrast, Luke had texted her earlier telling her what he'd had for breakfast. Another text from Vanessa had contained a photo of Tommy and Leanne grinning and waving while holding up drawings they'd made for their Aunty Clara.

Clara took it all in and concluded that there had never even been a choice to make. There was only one place for her if she wanted to be with people who cared about her and included her in their lives.

With her plan even more firmly in place, she worked tirelessly the next couple of days to get everything taken care of. Every loose end she handled opened up a Pandora's Box of an additional dozen loose ends she hadn't thought of. The fact that she had yet to contact a lawyer to find out where she stood legally concerning her name and nationality just made everything more difficult. However, having embraced both Eve and Clara, she was reluctant to choose between them. She would rather be both than just one.

She spoke with Duncan several times a day, but she didn't tell him she was coming home. She'd surprised everyone once and she intended to do it again. It would be a welcome do-over.

Ideally, she wanted to walk up to the Quinn door again to see if she was welcome, only this time with less fear. Not speaking to Grace and Carl made that part difficult, but then she'd just walk up to another Quinn door, Luke's maybe. Or the door she really wanted to always be open to her. The Cantwell one.

Two days before her flight, Clara collapsed onto her couch after a long day of packing and throwing stuff out. She had ordered a pizza, but after landing on the couch, she doubted she would have the energy to get up and answer the door when it was delivered.

Her thoughts drifted to Duncan. She missed him like crazy. They had barely talked or texted all day since both Emily and Peter had the flu, leaving everything at the studio to be handled by the boss alone. By the time he could call it a day, it would be deep into the night in Denmark and Clara would be fast asleep. A girl didn't need a better reason than that to relocate across the world—to be in the same time zone as the man she loved. Loved so much it hurt. She sighed. Two more days.

When the doorbell chimed, she did get up, but only because she knew it was for the sake of pizza. She was almost looking forward to the flight to America, knowing she could just lean back and relax.

Finding Clara

Back on the couch with her pizza and a glass of water, she groaned when the doorbell chimed again. Whoever it was, she wasn't sharing her dinner. Though, she couldn't think of anyone who would even want to. Apparently, the closest real friend was across the country.

Her jaw nearly hit the floor when she opened the door and saw Grace and Carl outside. If someone had told her to make a list of people who might be outside her door, Grace and Carl would have been right after the Hungarian minister of foreign affairs and a penguin from Antarctica.

Grace smiled tentatively. "Good evening, Clara."

"Hi. Um… Please come in." Standing back so they could walk into her moving box-cluttered apartment, she wondered why they were in Denmark. If they wanted to talk to her or maybe pressure her some more, they could have just picked up the phone instead of making such a long trip.

"Are you moving?" Carl asked as Clara was closing the door.

"Yes, as a matter of fact I am." She realized she was wearing her oldest jeans and a ratty T-shirt that she planned to throw away and sighed. Somewhere deep inside of her, there was a strange need to impress her parents. Ratty clothes weren't the way to accomplish that when they both looked stylish in their winter coats.

"Please sit down," she said, gesturing to the couch. "Can I get you anything?"

"No thanks. We just…" Grace looked at Carl, who continued. "We came to apologize and to get to know our daughter… On her home court so to speak."

Flabbergasted and more than a little overwhelmed, Clara sat down in her favorite reading chair, a chair currently filled with magazines, but she barely noticed. When the Quinns changed their minds, they did it in style. "I don't know what to say," she admitted.

"You don't have to say anything right now," Carl replied, the hint of a smile flashing before he turned serious again. "But will you listen?"

Clara nodded.

"Thank you. Even though we had twenty-seven years to imagine all the different outcomes of your kidnapping, Grace and I have had to accept that reality turned out to be quite another matter. Because we've become stubborn old fools, it's taken a long time to sink in. Too long. It's the worst thing we've ever done to any of our children and saying sorry isn't enough. But it's the only place we can start."

Grace moved away from Carl on the couch and patted the seat between them. "Please?"

Slowly, Clara stood up and sat down between her parents. Instantly, Grace reached for her hand.

"It's important that you understand, sweetie. Just because reality was different from what we'd imagined, it doesn't mean it was in any way disappointing. I'm afraid it might have come across that way. We were so hung up on names or I did at least, that we forgot to look beyond that. I got it into my head that because your name was Clara, you couldn't be my little girl and that's not true."

"We see you, Clara. We see you for you," Carl easily picked up where Grace left off, but there was nothing rehearsed about their words. "We love you. More than you will ever know. We won't try to push you into anything again. The baby who needed us for everything is gone, grown into an independent woman who doesn—"

"Who still needs you," Clara interrupted, seeing the truth in their words and realizing where she'd been wrong herself. "I think I've been hung up on names, too. In the sense, I didn't think there was room for both Eve and Clara. But that's not even the point, is it? I *am* Eve just as I *am* Clara. It's who I am."

She smiled at both her parents and took Carl's hand, too. "New start?"

They both nodded, looking just as overcome with emotion as Clara felt. This time, she was determined that they get it right.

"Thank you. That really means the world to me." She squeezed both their hands. "I was going to say that I was hoping you'd stay awhile so I could show you around and reveal more of my Danish side, but I'm actually headed back to Connecticut in a couple of days. I have a home there, you see. Emotionally, anyway."

Grace brought her in for a hug. "We'll come back here together. We do want to see where you grew up and all that, but it can wait."

"We brought you a present," Carl said after a moment. "Go open the door."

148

Hesitantly, Clara rose with a frown on her face.

"Go on," Grace encouraged her with a smile.

Not knowing what to think, she did as asked and had barely opened the door before she found herself enveloped in a pair of strong arms. She struggled against it for a second, but then she recognized the scent.

"Duncan!"

"God, I've missed you, baby. Never again." He loosened his grip and cupped her face with his cold hands. "I swear to God, never again."

"Never again," she agreed and stood on her toes to reach his equally cold lips. "I love you."

"Not as much as I love you."

The kiss was as intense as every hour had been boring and bland since she'd left Connecticut. She felt claimed as one hundred percent his when he pulled back to grin down at her.

"Best present ever," Clara commented, giddy with happiness.

Duncan laughed. "I thought they'd forgotten about me out here. They wanted to talk to you first. It was pure agony waiting. I almost went to see Gertrud instead."

She laughed. "Poor boy. Come inside. It's freezing out here."

He bent down to steal another kiss, though not as much 'stealing,' as she offered it willingly, before following her inside. When he saw the stacked boxes in the hallway, he stopped. "Going somewhere? Because, you know, wherever you go from now on, I'm totally tagging along. No more of this being in opposite corners of the world stuff. I don't care where I live, as long as it's the same place as you."

Clara looked at him, red-nosed from the cold and his eyes as serious as she'd ever seen them. He meant it. That was lucky since she meant it, too.

"I'm going home."

About the Author

Jannie Lund has been writing for as long as she's been able to spell—possibly longer—and she got her first short story published in 2008. It was a Christmas story that took a few hours to write, which gave her the impression that writing was easy. Later she found out how wrong she was. She dabbles in different genres and languages, but romance tends to be involved in one way or the other. Living in her native Denmark, she spends her non-writing time reading, enjoying nature in either running shoes or behind a camera lens, cooking and baking, and being creative in as many ways as possible.

www.jannielund.com
twitter@Jannielund
www.facebook.com/jannielundwriter
jalund@gmail.com
www.goodreads.com/author/show/6457105.Jannie_Lund

Other Works by the Author with Melange Books

A Thousand Sunsets

Printed in Great Britain
by Amazon